CHOSEN TO BE MINE

A Dark Arranged Marriage Mafia Romance

Jolie Damman

"There are many types of marriage relationships and all of them can work, but none is sadder than the one that doesn't represent peace in your heart."

— SHANNON L. ALDER

CONTENTS

CHAPTER 1

The Chase

Alide

I put on my running shoes and looked around. Ahhhh, Central Park wasn't in its best conditions, but it still looked scenic. The small hills painted the landscape, the trees were almost leafless, and the squirrels were running around.

One of them, who was approaching me, bolted to a tree, where it hid. A pity, I presumed. I was pondering getting it in my hands. It was a childhood dream of mine.

"Alide, do you really have to go jogging right now?" Rita asked.

She was behind me, sitting on a bench. I gave her a look of 'I'm not going to change my mind' and started to warm up. I kicked the air with my knees multiple times, and then spun my arms before stretching them. A gush of wind kissed my thighs. I shivered. I knew Fall was here already, but I didn't think it was going to be this cold. Should have known better, considering we were in New York and it was one of the chilliest cities in the country. A hand tugged my tight pants for jogging. I snapped my head down and said, "Luca, what do you want?"

"I want to pee," he said with a feeble voice. I stopped stretching my right leg and put my hands on my waist, my heart going from 80 to 8 in seconds. Even though he was ruining my routine, I didn't hate him. How could I? He was so little and loveable.

My lips curved up to form a tight-lipped smile, and I put my hand on his back. "Come on, big boy. I'm taking you to the restroom."

We descended a set of stairs and reached the public restroom. In the middle of the region which delimited it was the statue of an angel. It was made of metal – copper maybe. My eyes scanned the skyline, the buildings, the people, and I thought: how much better could this city get? There was no place quite like it. Well, maybe Chicago was similar, but I hadn't had a chance to visit it yet.

"Here we go, big boy. I'm going with you to the door, and then you'll do your thing by yourself, okay?"

He coughed and nodded. As he walked to the men's section of the restroom, I couldn't help but think how much he worried me. He was supposed to be taller than that. He was 13 and had a lot of growing up to do, but still... he looked more like he was 8.

And I couldn't believe our father left him alone with me... I rested on a pillar that supported the entrance of the main restroom structure, and watched as people walked here and there. Not much going on in Central Park. There was the distant sound of traffic and the occasional plane flying to the JFK Airport, but other than those things, not much was happening. One could almost forget we lived in a city with over eight million people living in it. I bolted my eyes shut and was thinking about how I could better find a job when a hand tugged my running pants again. I smiled upon looking down and going on one knee. I loved my little brother so much I'd do anything for him.

Luca's face was so pale, though. I wished I could know what was going on with him. I had a suspicion, but didn't share it with him or Rita yet. I didn't want to worry them more than they already were.

I caressed his forehead and said, "Are you going to be fine with Rita? She cares about you. She's great."

He intersected his arms over his chest when I withdrew my hand. "But sis, I wanna play with *you*." I sighed. "I will play with you, just not right now." I paused. "Come, I'll take you back to Rita. She's probably devouring an ice cream right now as we speak." We avoided people jogging and having fun with their partners as we made our way back to the bench. It was by a small newspaper kiosk. I asked myself who still bought those things in this day and age before having to push the question away.

I had just seen Rita, and she, indeed, was devouring an ice-cream.

She padded to us, her legs a reflection of how she had nothing to worry about. She was my caretaker and all, but that didn't impede me from judging her when I had to. It wasn't long ago she gave me and Luca a big scare, after all.

That night... when she had an AVC and her whole body went lifeless...

I could never forget it.

A tear menaced to come out. I couldn't remember those things right now. It wasn't good. Her belly bounced as much as her legs moved while she approached us, her eyes focused on the vanilla and chocolate ice-cream only, as if it was the most delicious thing in the universe.

I put my hands on my waist when she stopped in front of us. She was going to have to explain herself to me. Her eyes slowly spun up, and they broadened when she realized I had already come back. My posture and expression probably made her understand what was going on in my mind right now.

"Alide, it's *just* one ice-cream."

"It's not, Rita." I paused. "It's much more than that. It can kill you, like it almost did that day."

Another moment of quietness as she remembered what happened that night. She was going to launch a firework – which was one of those not-too-loud ones that explode in a delightful light spectacle in the sky – when her eyes rolled inside her head and she toppled over. I had concluded, for sure, that was the end of her. It was a good thing we managed to get to the hospital in time. I couldn't remember the face of the man who found me screaming as loud as I could by the sidewalk, but I wished I did. I didn't even have time to thank him for his kindness before he drove off.

Rita sighed and expressed, "Well, I'm not going to waste this ice-cream."

I shook my head. "You should have bought a gelato at least. It's much better than this stuff the Americans make."

"The closest gelato shop I know is in Little Italy, and I'm not going there just for it." She paused. "Now, if you will excuse me." A long look of dissatisfaction followed. "I've got an ice-cream to finish."

With her hand still holding the cone, she sashayed back to the bench like what I had just said mattered nothing to her. I wasn't scorning her for eating ice-cream, I swear. I just wanted to tell her to be cautious. I didn't know what Luca and I would do without her. Luca tugged my pants again, and I craned my head to look at him. "What do you want this time, little one?"

He pouted his lips, looking irritated. "I'm not little anymore."

"That's not what I asked, and it's irrelevant right now. I want to know what you want."

"To go to the zoo with you again. I want to see the other animals and stuff..."

I got on one knee one more time, and peered at his eyes. "We'll go there soon. Not right now, but we'll go there." I paused, pondering if I was going to have time to jog in the park and take him to the zoo.

"Okay, we'll go there once I've finished jogging. How does that sound?" I continued.

As if by a miracle, his eyes lit up. "You promise?"

I messed his hair. "I promise."

I straightened back up and continued, "Now, stay with Rita. I'm coming back in a bit."

"Yes, ma'am!" He said, joy in his tone.

His legs took him as fast as possible to Rita, who smiled and bulged her eyes when she noticed him coming to her at full speed. They were so adorable when they were having fun, I thought before scanning the path I was going to follow. *Go to the right, then the left, and continue along that hill, then take the right and follow the lake until you are back here.*

Central Park wasn't too complex. It was overestimated by many tourists who came here. The movies brainwashed them about it, I thought before warming up once more. One two, three and four, I began to count before stretching my right arm, twisting my torso and kicking the air with my knees multiple times to get ready to jog. I could already feel the temperature of my body rising.

With Luca being taken care of by Rita, I could finally exercise, and I needed to keep myself in shape.

With that reflection in mind, I hopped ahead. The hop then turned into a slow, measured jog.

No need to push myself too hard doing this.

I curved a portion of the lake, went through a path along the zoo, spotted some birds flying toward the Empire State building, witnessed some squirrels as they mated, and contemplated some couples while they kissed in public. Nothing out of the usual here. There were even people jogging with me. I could forget about my life troubles while doing this. Being unemployed, having no life future to speak of, not knowing who my father really was, Luca and his current condition, Rita's obesity, and all the other things which worried me...

And that's when I spotted a couple having an argument.

It was a man with short blond hair and a woman with a red coat. Their discussion was fiery. People kept glancing at them, probably asking themselves why the hell they weren't taking their quarrel somewhere else. And me being me, inquisitive as always, I couldn't help but halt right beside them.

"I can't take being with you anymore! I can't take a stroll with a friend of mine without you thinking I'm cheating on you!" The woman shouted, her cheeks red like lava.

Jesus. Maybe I shouldn't be here.

But, too late now, I supposed when the couple's heads snapped in my direction.

"What are you doing here?" The man asked, spilling his hatred at me.

"I'm just curious. Why are you arguing?"

Oh fuck, that was a dreadful question. I shouldn't have worded it like that.

"Does it matter?" The woman rebuked, making me flinch and think, once again, why the hell did I even decide to meddle with their shit. Did I think I could help these people or what?

"No... I guess it doesn't..." I apologized, walking away from there with both of my hands in front of me, making a shield of sorts.

The man threw his finger at her face and their heated, loud discussion recommenced. Some people shook their heads, probably thinking I shouldn't have involved myself. I was thinking the same thing, to be honest. *Grrrr.* Why did I think I could have done anything about their dispute? Stop being nosy, Alide, I thought to myself before resuming my jogging.

The wind kept brushing my face as I jogged along the main lake, watching the cars as they went down the roads, the people in the balconies of their apartments, and the planes while they ascended in the overcast sky.

One of my dreams was to visit Italy. My family was from there, but we were pretty poor here. I just wished so much to get to know Rome, Milan and the Vatican.

That's when, all of a sudden, my eyes picked up some dollar bills in the grass. There were three of them, and they looked legit. They didn't look like those dollar bills found in toy sets. Those looked as fake as they could be. Those in the grass, though, had to be from someone who had lost them somehow.

I stopped, looked around, and squatted by the dollar bills. I picked them up and scanned the park once more. I knew I shouldn't be worried, but my heart was in my throat nonetheless. What if the dollar bills were from a dangerous man?

Also, what if he then intended to kill me? That's not something I wanted to find myself in. The last thing I needed was someone hunting me down because of his money. I peeked around again, my head going from 0 to almost 180 degrees leisurely. I perused the whole area, watched the people near me – and also the ones far away – before making a decision.

Despite being poor and Luca needing his medicine, I wasn't about to steal money from someone who'd lost it. Maybe the person who dropped these bills really needed them and was going to come back here... eventually. Perhaps, someone else was going to come here and snatch these bills instead of me. Whatever was going to happen, it wasn't my problem.

It was with that consideration in mind I stood up and continued my jogging. No point trying to be the hero or the villain when I could barely live as things were. And if I were to succeed in life, it would be through my own merits, after all.

I recalled some of the instances Rita said I never worried about anything. Little did she know that wasn't true. I was with my heart in my throat the whole time when I had those bills in my hands. I almost thought they were cursed or something. And I definitely made the right choice.

Angelo

I took a deep breath and opened the door to my father's office. I had been here many times before, but still had to take in the details of it another time. The portraits hung from the walls. They bore photos and moments of me, dad and my little brother. *Vinicio... I never thought things would turn out the way they did to you*, I speculated before my throat clogged up. *Not now*, I advised myself. *Don't make father think you feel sorry for him, or else he will ask his men to kill you as well. He's paranoid. He thinks everyone's a traitor.*

His office was quite old school. It didn't have a window; just one AC unit to bring the air in and out. Everything – or better, almost everything – was made of hardwood, and the dominant color of the place was a medium tone of brown. He had a warm, orange-ish table lamp for his studies, and on his desk were a bunch of documents and other sheets of paper. He didn't use a computer, and to be frank, he didn't need one. Despite being paranoid to the point of killing some of his men when one of them as much as looked at him the wrong way, he was smart.

No wonder he managed to build the family the way it was now and avoid the authorities, who for sure were still looking for enough evidence to jail him. The door closed behind me with a gentle thud. Dad raised his head and said, "Son, I've heard Vinicio was spotted in Central Park. Ask Prudenzio for details. He will tell you everything you need to know."

His words disconcerted me.

"But dad, is there nothing that can change your mind? Vinicio is my younger brother. I still care about him..."

He banged the desk. "*Enough of that, Angelo*. I taught you better than this. Vinicio is a traitor. He will pay for the choice he made."

"But how can you say that?! He hasn't ratted you out to the cops."

A moment of hiatus as his cold and yet, fiery eyes locked with mine again. "He chose his path. You know what happened, *and I'm not going to repeat myself*." I shook my head and walked out of there, not believing I had to put up with this shit. I really wished to make father understand Vinicio did nothing of what he's accusing him of. I then walked through the part of the restaurant where we had the tables, and the guests were already coming in. Some of them greeted me, and I greeted them back. I guessed they knew who I was. By being the Don's underboss, people here respected me, and my actions, so far, had been speaking for themselves. These people here feared me more than anything, to be honest.

I strode out of the restaurant. The sign, which was a plaque with letters painted in green, white and red – the colors of the Italian flag – hung just above the entrance. People were still coming in for their pizzas and other Italian delicacies. My father wasn't only good at running shady operations, he was also an expert on making his restaurant flourish here in New York. Little Italy would never be the same without him and the Bello Italiano.

My eyes registered another sign. It was just at the entrance of the neighborhood. *Welcome to Little Italy*, it read. The welcome part brought a smile to my face. *Welcome* was not an appropriate word for this neighborhood. It should be more like *STAY THE FUCK AWAY*. Prudenzio was leaning against his black sedan, ready to take me to Central Park. "Tell me everything I need to know," I demanded upon stopping in front of him.

He nodded and explained to me all the details.

He brought his phone to me and showed me the photos. That was Vinicio alright. I ran my hand over my face. I couldn't believe I was about to do this again. The only thing I could hope for was Vinicio outsmarting me again. I didn't want to bring him to our dad. I knew what he would do to him, and I would never be able to live with myself if he accomplished it...

Nevertheless, maybe his fate could be different. Father was old and he gave us some scares already. There was even this one day he had a heart attack. It was doubtful anyone would kill him, but since he was nearing 70 years of age, there was a good chance he was going to die soon. Vinicio only needed to leave the city somehow, or wait until our dad passed away.

Prudenzio drove through the city as fast as he could, overtaking some cars without breaking the laws of traffic. He was an excellent driver, and we were taking two more soldiers with us. We didn't need many *soldati* to find Vinicio. I knew he was alone. He was just a man running for his life. He was no Mafia man, and he couldn't be one. That's one of the many reasons he ran away.

Prudenzio pulled over by Central Park. His hand reached for his Colt, and I nodded. It was time to do this. No matter how much pain this was going to inflict on me, I wasn't about to fail father. I slipped out of the car and headed to the direction the photos were taken from. He was last spotted near Central Park's restrooms. The place could be identified from a distance. It was big and some angel statues made of bronze stood in front of it.

It was cold here too, so we had to put on some layers before reaching the park. Thanks to the lower temperatures, not many people were visiting the locale, which was a good thing. I didn't want many witnesses talking to the police later on. My eyes then suddenly caught sight of a superb lady with a little boy and a woman who I assumed to be her mother. They were standing by the lake, chatting and laughing.

I wished I could be like them right now, I thought.

I nodded to Prudenzio again. "You and you," I instructed, pointing my finger at them. "Take that route. Scout the place. If you spot him, shoot at the sky. Prudenzio and I will then go to you as fast as we can."

They nodded, their eyes serious and attentive.

Good, I thought. I needed soldiers I could trust, and those two were some of the best.

Prudenzio and I trotted to the main area of the restrooms. We were going there as fast as we could without drawing attention to us. Someone who had no idea who we were was probably thinking we were nothing more than friends coming to take a stroll in the park. I reached the front of the restroom, and just as I'd expected, Vinicio wasn't here. The man who recognized him had followed him, but then, ended up losing him. I was kind of glad he did. I didn't want anyone other than me getting him.

I perused the surrounding environment, and that's when I spotted him.

Just behind some trees, eating what seemed to be a Philly cheesesteak...

The sight of it brought me memories I thought I had long forgotten.

I pointed my Colt to the sky and squeezed the trigger. The shot caused people to panic and run. Birds flew away. "I found him! Let's go!" I bolted to him, Prudenzio following me. Maybe I shouldn't have shot, but it didn't matter anyway. Close to Vinicio were my two other soldiers, and they were going to surround him.

And he had now no chance of escaping this. The moment I steered my gun at my brother and they spotted him was when I realized that this was it. I was going to get my younger brother, and then... who knew what was going to happen to him?

I guessed my hope was that my father would realize he was still his son and would pardon him somehow. My men sprinted so fast Vinicio wasn't able to finish his Philly cheesesteak. He dropped it and put his hands in front of him, forming a shield.

"Brother, y-you don't have to do this."

"I have. Come peacefully, and father will forgive you. I give you my word."

"But he won't!"

A moment of silence. I was going to approach him and bring him to our father anyway when, all of a sudden, someone grabbed me and threw me down to the grass with her or him. I heard shouts, people running, shots being fired, and when I spun to meet who had done that to me, I saw the face of a magnificent woman. Her hair was straight, dark brown, and her eyes were of the same color, but with a lighter tone.

Her face was angelic. It had no defects. Her lips were full, and I found myself in some kind of weird trance. Her eyes locked with mine, and for a moment, neither of us did anything. I stood there, dumbfounded as my mind barely registered the sound of a bicycle riding to the other side of the stone path I was near to.

A tempest of a thought crossed my mind.

Vinicio. I stood up in a flash, almost making her topple as she also stood up.

My head jerked repeatedly, following different directions, trying to find my brother, but he was nowhere to be seen. My men couldn't be found as well. Whatever happened, it seemed I'd lost him once more, and it was all because of *her*. And wait... Wasn't she the one I'd spotted by the lake with the little boy and her mother minutes ago? Another wild thought crossed my mind. Those facial sketches, those eyes, that nose... I knew her. Fuck. What the hell was this? Some kind of sick joke?

She approached me, her body exhaling her uncomfortableness. Her hands didn't know what to do with each other.

"Hey, I'm sorry I pushed you with me on the ground. There was this crazy old man on a bike and he was going to hit you. I just thought I had to, you know, save you..."

Alide.

She chuckled, like she knew she was to blame. I had no time or the patience to find this funny. She didn't finish her sentence, but I knew what she meant. "It's fine," I said before scanning the hills, the trees, the buildings and the roads once more. No signs of them. No shouting, people screaming, or running away. Just another attempt to get Vinicio back that was squandered, I presumed before tucking my Colt into my waistband.

I then proceeded to walk back to the car. Maybe Alide wanted to tell me something more, and maybe she even recognized me. It didn't matter to me, and so I kept my mouth shut. Truth was, I had no time for her right now. I needed to find Prudenzio and tell my father how things went here.

CHAPTER 2

Hired

Alide

He walked away without as much as thanking me. Who was he, and why did he have a gun? I had no idea what his name was, but he looked handsome. He was taller than me. His hair was a deep tone of black, with a thick stubble on his chiseled face, and his body was athletic without being overly muscular.

I couldn't help but admire him as he made his way out of Central Park. I thought he was going to feel thankful I saved him from getting hurt. I swear people in this park needed to pay more attention to where they were going. How come someone allowed that crazy old man to ride his bicycle around here without watchful eyes over him all the time? I sighed and walked out of there. Whoever that man was, he was way beyond my league. And he seemed pretty serious and tight, like he couldn't have fun even if his life depended on it. He was a man of few words, and he didn't like wasting time with anything.

I knew what Rita would say about him. *He's the opposite of you.* I walked back to her and Luca. His eyes fired up when he saw me coming. He ran up to me and then jumped. I held him by his armpits, not believing how light he was. His face was so pale, despite the pink tone of his cheeks. I needed to do something about his condition and most of all, I needed to find a job. That was the only way to make sure he would have a normal life one day.

I put him down and Rita inquired, "What happened back there?"

"Oh, the shots?" I said, almost not believing that witnessing gunshots turned into such a common thing for me. *Living in Brooklyn will do that to you*, I opined before responding, "Nothing of importance. Don't worry about it." She stood up and dusted off the front of her skirt. "Well, if you are done jogging, then we can go back home now. I don't want to miss Westworld tonight."

I gave her a look of dissatisfaction, not accepting she still watched that piece of shit. Her hands gave off her embarrassment as she declared, "I'm not going to stop watching it. It's good. You should give it another go." "Maybe another time, in another life," I said as we left Central Park. Tomorrow I was going to have to return to Lower Manhattan to go job-hunting again. I sighed internally.

I couldn't believe finding a job was so hard in 2020.

* * *

The bus pulled over by the sidewalk and I slipped out. A gush of wind tossed my hair in the other direction. Good thing I still had papà's coat, I thought before heading over to the entrance of the neighborhood. The sign which hung between two buildings read in cursive letters 'Little Italy.' Yup, this is Little Italy.

I could find all sorts of food and Italian stuff here. Still, I was sure it was all Americanized, so it was nothing quite like experiencing the real stuff in Italy. One day, I said to myself again, I was going to travel over there. I entered the neighborhood and stopped in front of the first restaurant which caught my attention. *Bello Italiano*, the sign just above the front door, read. I peeped inside it through the large, front windows. People were chatting and having lunch in there, I thought before considering if this place was worth a shot.

I looked around and presumed this was as good as any place.

I crept open the door of the establishment and stepped in. None of the customers paid attention to me. A man, about my height and with long, dark hair presented himself. He had a menu and a notepad in his hands. He wore a typical waiter's attire, and his mouth opened to make me a question, "Miss, do you want a table for one?" "No, I'm not here to eat." I paused, thinking. "I'm here searching for work. I saw the job posting online." He blinked, his eyes clearing up. "Oh, right." He paused, eyes darting to the upper right for a moment. "Come right this way. The boss is here."

I knew he would be, or almost knew. He mentioned coming around this time of the day, after all. The waiter took me to the back section of the establishment, where I couldn't hear the chatter and laughter of the customers anymore. This was where all the niceness of the Bello Italiano died. In here, the walls weren't painted, and there was dust everywhere.

I could only hope, if he hired me, that he was going to make me work as a waitress *only*. I couldn't imagine myself cleaning all these walls and floors.

The man stopped in front of a grey door. He knocked on it and said it was him. Another man, whose voice was much deeper and older, declared, "Come on in." The waiter had already mentioned it was someone coming for an interview, so the boss already knew why I had come. He then opened the door and stepped aside, allowing me in. He shut it the moment my eyes landed on an old man who was sitting behind his desk. His hair was grey and thinning, and his office was very old school.

He had some portraits hanging from the walls, with most of them depicting him and who I could only imagine to be his sons. None of the portraits was crooked, and the space was the cleanest and tidiest thing I had seen inside this back partition of his restaurant. He offered me to sit on the chair in front of his desk with his hand. "Let's see if we can find a position for you here."

I sat and said, "If you don't mind, I would rather work as a waitress, like the job posting online cited..."

His eyes studied me, and I felt he had a sudden moment of realization, like seeing me brought him memories back. Whatever was the case, his expression made me feel like running the fuck away from here as fast as possible.

Despite that, I thought back Luca and decided to stay.

"Oh, right. If you don't mind, we've got some basic things to go over here. Do you have your resume with you?"

I pulled it out of my suitcase and put it down on his desk, relieved that I'd considered printing some copies of it, just in case. I hadn't thought they would come in handy, taking into account this was 2020 and many people favored their documents in the digital format, but it seemed I was wrong.

He picked up the resume and glanced over it. During the entire time we spoke about my objectives – how I could contribute to the restaurant, and all that bullshit – I had this weird feeling like he knew me and was taking it easy with me. It couldn't be the case, right?

He couldn't know me. It was the first time I was ever seeing him, after all.

He and I stood up. "Welcome to the Bello Italiano. You'll work as a waitress, just like the job posting... errr... online, said," he uttered, throwing his hand in front of him to tell me he couldn't be bothered with where I'd found the ad. I smiled and bowed. "Thank you very much, Mr. Romani." He rounded the table and walked with me to the door. "Someone here will tell you the ins and outs, teach you what you need to know and that sort of thing. You don't have to worry about how to start."

He waited and then continued, "Is it okay for you to begin working here tomorrow?"

There was a paternal tone in his voice, but I took it as him being so old he couldn't help but see me as the daughter he never had – if he had one, I was sure there would have been at least a dozen of her portraits in his office, after all.

"Yes, that's okay. Thank you very much again."

The corner of his lip curved up to form a gentle smirk and the door opened. And in stepped *none other than the guy who I'd saved back in Central Park!* He stood immense as he did back then, and he wore a dark suit very similar to the one he had put on before. His eyes found mine, and he blinked like he couldn't believe he was seeing me here. I flickered my eyelids as well. I had no idea I was going to find him here, and unless he was looking for a job, which I didn't think he was, that meant... he was one of Mr. Romani's sons!

Talk about New York being too small, I thought, still feeling as if my heart was going to burst out of my chest.

And no wonder I couldn't recognize him when I'd glanced over the portraits on the walls. His face looked different. In front of me was standing a grown man. In the pictures, he was much younger. His eyes finally unlocked with mine, and I didn't know what to say. I thought about giving the boss another good impression of me by greeting his son, but all that came out of my mouth were only incoherent noises. Seeing what was happening, Mr. Romani put his hand on my back and the other on his son's. "Ahhhh, Angelo." A moment of pause as he glanced at me, and then at his son. "This is our new waitress. Her name is Alide, and she will be working with us from tomorrow onwards."

His eyes blinked once more, but his expression remained unchanged. The novelty of having found me here had worn off, I imagined. He presented his hand to me, and for a moment, I didn't know what to do with it. Then, I shook it and commented, "Nice to meet you. I'm Alide Mazzanti."

I still got the impression from him that he knew me somehow. He seemed surprised I showed up here, but telling him my name made him express nothing. It was like he, undeniably, knew who I was.

I withdrew my hand the moment he did the same. I'd felt how powerful his grip was. I knew we had no chance of ever becoming more than what we were to each other, but still... a girl could dream and, right now, I was dreaming a bit too much. Rita would have all sorts of things to tell me about not to approach the boss's fine-looking son and to keep a professional relationship with him, I thought with an internal smile.

I closed my eyes, grinning, and then declared, "I have to go now, but it was good meeting you." Mr. Romani grabbed my hand gently and made me stop. "You don't want a ride back home?"

For a moment, I didn't know how to respond. It was the first time an employer had ever offered me something like that. I glimpsed at him and his son. The latter looked serious and uptight. That was his usual self. I wondered if he had many friends.

I chuckled fretfully as he ungripped my hand. "Okay, sure. Why not, right?"

"Ahhhh." His eyes lit up like a bonfire. "Angelo, get your car and take her home."

Oh shit. I'd reckoned he himself was going to take me home, not his son. I hadn't thought this moment could have become more uncomfortable, but it just did. Angelo didn't sigh, like I was expecting him to. One second later, he said, "Okay, but we'll talk later, *papà*."

His father's expression grew serious, eyebrows narrowing. And instead of promising him they were going to have a conversation, he merely turned and walked back to his desk. A lot was spoken without words when their eyes were locked to each other, I guessed.

I toddled to the hallway and Angelo closed the door behind him. Without saying anything, he walked to the other way of the hall and took me to the back of the establishment, where they had a tiny parking space. His car was a pitch-black Chrysler. I couldn't remember what the exact model was, but it was the one with a round grille and headlights. Again, without disclosing as much as a word, he opened the front door by the passenger seat, and closed it after I sat.

He then opened the other door and drove the car through the narrow alleyway that led to their parking spot. He didn't say this, but I knew that parking space was for him and his family only. I imagined they lived in the rooms above the restaurant too, so he probably had more family than his father - like his brother in the photographs, and a mother. Was initiating a conversation with him the right thing to do? Probably, definitely, I thought before opening my mouth, "So... you work for your father?"

"You could say that," he said before rounding a corner and taking another road. The Brooklyn bridge loomed in the distance.

I assumed he was going to say something else, but as the seconds went by and we neared the bridge further, I concluded otherwise.

With that consideration in mind, I decided to make him another query, "What were you doing in the park that day?"

"Nothing. Don't worry about it." He paused. "Thanks for saving me from that bike, by the way."

Wow.

I didn't think he would say that, but I still couldn't help but smile and say, "It was just the right thing to do."

"I know. It's good to have people who care about strangers," he spoke before entering another road. The Brooklyn bridge was within walking distance now, and I could see more cars following us.

As we neared it, I asked, "I couldn't help but notice you have a brother when I was in your father's office..."

It was nothing more than a simple statement – just something I threw in the air to see how he would respond.

Angelo shrugged and said, "He's alright."

And *He's alright* was all he dared to tell me, like he had nothing more about his brother he could share. He was a reserved man for sure, and all of a sudden, I found myself wishing I could fast forward time. I tried initiating another friendly conversation with him, but it was clear Angelo wasn't willing to talk about anything. He pulled over after I said this was the road I lived in, and when I opened the door, I said, "Thanks for taking me here."

"Don't mention it," he said before driving ahead and rounding the corner back to lower Manhattan.

I stood there, contemplating he was a fine-looking man with a big problem. If only he could be more friendly and not from a completely different world than mine, than I could have a chance with him. However, as things stood, he was just beyond me.

I turned and opened the door to our little home. Luca was sitting on his couch, his fingers playing with his phone. Rita was in the kitchen, and the smell of gnocchi was unmistakable. Luca raised his head and didn't run to me as I was expecting him to. He coughed and put his phone down on the sofa. I sped to him, put my suitcase on the couch, and got on one knee so that my eyes were level with his.

"I've got the best news ever!"

His eyes lit up, though only a little. Rita said from behind me, "What kind of good news? Did you finally get a job?" I nodded, warping up a corner of my lips. She threw the handkerchief she was using to dry her hands over her head, and it landed on her colorful curlers. "I can't believe it!"

I bowed again, feeling a surge of warmth in my heart. Telling them the good news was better than hearing Mr. Romani telling me I had been hired.

I turned my head to Luca, whose cheeks blushed again. "That means I can finally buy a PS4!" he beamed, fisting one hand and punching the air with it. "Not so fast, little one," I said, ruffling his hair. "I need to buy your medicine first."

His eyes lost some of the initial energy, and upon witnessing that, I reaffirmed, "But, I'll buy your PS4 soon. It's pretty cheap. Just wait a month, okay?"

"Yes, ma'am!" He said energetically, nodding once quickly. He proceeded to sprint to the backyard, where I hoped he was going to have a good time. I stood up with a silly smirk on my face. There was nothing quite like making him feel happy.

I was going to buy him that PS4, that I swore. Rita padded to me as she removed the handkerchief which landed on her head. "Where are you going to work at?"

"The Bello Italiano in Little Italy. It's an Italian restaurant."

Her handkerchief fell from her hands as her eyes went wide.

"What happened?" I was forced to ask.

Something about the name of the establishment made her have a sudden, inopportune moment of realization. She wasn't going to ask me not to work there for whatever reason, was she?

Her voice was nothing more than a whisper when she spoke, "I've heard terrible things about that place..."

Did she? Was she telling the truth? The air grew thicker all of a sudden.

"What kind of things?"

"Isn't it obvious? It's Little Italy. It's where the Mafia operates from. Didn't you say the man you saved yesterday had a gun with him in fucking Central Park?"

She had no idea he also was from there and worked for his father, or had she?

Was there something else she wasn't telling me?

"Rita, if there's something I need to know..."

A moment of stillness as her eyes continued to study me. "No, there's nothing," she finally enunciated.

"Are you sure?"

She picked up the handkerchief and when she raised her head, her expression was one of gentleness. "Yeah, pretty sure."

She padded to me and put a hand on my shoulder as she then led me to the kitchen. "It's nothing. I was just worried about you for a second." She paused. "Little Italy is in lower Manhattan, but it's still a dangerous place." I had no idea if I should believe her or not, though the impression that she was hiding something from me remained. Or was that just me thinking too much about something as simple as Rita being concerned?

Shit. I had no idea any longer. Better to pretend that what just happened didn't, I opined before giving her an uncomfortable smirk. Mr. Romani seemed nice enough. If something bizarre or treacherous happened in his restaurant, then I could simply fire myself. As I looked out the window to where Luca was playing with his phone in the backyard, I reaffirmed my goal to make sure we were going to have enough money for his medicine. I needed that job so fucking much.

CHAPTER 3

Properly Meeting Alide

Angelo

Anger was rising within my heart. I couldn't believe my father had hired her. Of all the people he could have chosen as our next waitress, why her? Was he playing some kind of sick game with me? She was lovely, angelic, and sweet. She wasn't a woman for the kind of world we lived in, and the more I kept it hidden that I was aware of who she was, the worst things seemed to become to me. I ran my hand over my face. "Father, I'm not going to marry her."

"There is a vow!" He shouted, banging the desk with his hand.

"And what of it? I don't owe anything to her father."

He trotted to me and gripped the collar of my shirt, his eyes burning with an intense hatred as they locked with mine. "You *will* respect the vow, and the marriage *is* going to happen."

He ungripped my shirt, and I didn't unwrinkle it.

"Her father was a good friend of mine. The best! I'm not going to allow his memory to become nothing. You will marry her, and you will be a good spouse."

A moment of pause, and then, he prolonged, "If not for you, then do it for me."

I sighed, knowing I wasn't going to change his mind right now. There was no way a marriage with Alide was ever going to work. She was so different, so much *not like me*. We wouldn't last a month.

Why did she have to arise all of a sudden in my life again?

There was another woman who I'd rather marry. I hadn't met her often these last few years, but she knew who I was. *She understood me.* She was no novice to the Mafia world. Her father had been trying to convince mine to let us marry each other, but it appeared it hadn't led to anything.

"About Vinicio..." I said, changing the subject. And God, did I need to talk about something different right now.

"You squandered it again," father said, waving his hand as if to tell me he didn't care. It was a lie. He cared.

"Maybe you should know that Alide was involved."

He snapped his head to me. "Involved? How?"

"I had him, in the park. Then, out of nowhere, she pushed me because apparently a cyclist was going to hit me or something." He raised an eyebrow. "At least, that's what she told me."

I paced in front of him. "By the time I got up, my men and Prudenzio were already gone. He said Vinicio disappeared before he could chase him. We'll have to wait until he shows up again." He shook his head, maybe telling me he didn't believe any of what I'd said. Maybe he was thinking I had come up with that excuse to make him hate Alide and push away the blame from me.

Whatever he was thinking about, I didn't care. I told him the truth.

"Fine, my son." He sat purposefully on his chair. "Just make sure it doesn't happen again, and I'm going to tighten up security at our checkpoints. Vinicio can't escape."

I walked out of his office and proceeded to my bedroom, where I then collapsed on the bed. I closed my eyes and began to think. If I were to marry Alide for sure, I wasn't going to be able to give my father a nephew or niece. I didn't want to think this, but I did so anyway. *Good thing he's old and dying.*

Alide

I arrived at the restaurant and was introduced to the ins and outs of my job in it by the same waiter who'd welcomed me when I first set foot in here. He was friendly and very welcoming. I couldn't stop smiling as he explained to me what to do whenever a customer got angry, needed something we didn't have, broke a glass, or thought the bill was too high. He explained everything while cracking jokes and smiling as well. He was a good man, and I found myself presuming this could be the right job for me.

And most of all, I needed to make sure the boss was going to be happy with me here. I needed the money for Luca's medicine, and then, once I had saved up enough,

I was thinking of taking him to a shrink or something like that. He didn't seem normal, and he was making me think he had depression or something just as bad.

Time passed, and I took Fantino's advice to heart. They helped me quite a bit. The customers of the Bello Italiano could be quite temperamental, depending on the thing that bothered them. By the time I was done serving them on my first day, I was exhausted and sweating with damp armpits. Fantino stopped in front of me, his eyebrows narrowing. "Do you think you can tidy up Mr. Angelo's room? The maid they hired for that wasn't able to come today. I know your job isn't to do that sort of thing, but I have to go now. Otherwise, I'd do it." He paused, breathing in. "It shouldn't take more than thirty minutes."

"Ahhh, sure thing, I guess. I'll do it."

He gave me a gentle smirk. "Great. Knew I could count on you."

Fantino padded me on the shoulder a couple of times, grabbed his stuff and walked out of the establishment after taking off his work attire to put on his everyday clothes. I looked upstairs, thinking my day could be ending a lot better right now if I didn't have to do any room cleaning. I sighed, went to the tiny room, took the cleaning equipment with me, and then walked to the last floor of the building, where Angelo's room was supposed to be.

I felt like I was invading his privacy, but if he were to find me here, he would probably not feel bothered. There was nothing to worry about, but still, I couldn't stop fantasizing about him. I drooled over Angelo. He looked self-assured, walked with the posture of a man who knew what he wanted and, as far as I knew, he also didn't have a girlfriend.

I wished though, more than anything right now, that the other waiters and waitresses hadn't gone back home yet. I began to sweep the room with a large broom, and there wasn't much to do here. It was all well organized, for the most part.

There was a thick sheet of dust all over the furniture and the floor, though, which suggested that the room wasn't used often. I wondered what he did most of his days.

Was Rita right about him being a member of the Mafia?

I hope not, was my thought when I looked around and concluded there were few things left to do here. I checked the time on my phone and found out that not even twenty minutes had passed since I'd entered his room. That was terrific. It meant I was undoubtedly not going to miss my bus back home. The way his room was decorated – if one could even say that about it – told me that not only Angelo was a man with excessive self-esteem, but that he also didn't care much about what was expensive and what was cheap. His TV was large, but the bed was quite simple, despite being king-sized. The wallpaper was a faded shade of blue. His laptop computer was old. It basically could do all he needed, and that was that.

He probably didn't use it to play games or watch movies in 4k. He was a very technical, efficient and... dare I say *boring* kind of man.

The only thing that kept making me drool over him, despite its irrationality, was his looks (and his excessive self-esteem, though they kind of went together, so it wasn't like I could separate them). I was wiping the top of his dresser with a handkerchief when my elbow hit a small, gold-decorated box. It fell on the floor, much to my shock and fright.

I assumed I had broken it before realizing it was made of cardboard. *Phew,* I thought before going on my knees to pick it up.

That's when I noticed a weird, alarming photo. Angelo was in it, and he wasn't alone. His father and who I assumed to be his brother – the same guy I saw surrounded by him and his men in Central Park before – were with him.

They were in a dark basement, and their facial features were almost indiscernible, but I was still sure it was them.

There was another man in the middle of the room, and he had been beaten up almost to a pulp. His head was lolled to one side, there was a huge lump where his left eye should be, his whole body was covered with bruises and cuts, and there was also a line of blood coming from a corner of his mouth. And perhaps, the most shocking thing was that they were all smiling at the camera. All of them, except for the younger brother, who looked disgusted and frightened by the whole scene. I turned the photo around and found some writings on it.

December 25th, 2010, in our tiny and adorable basement.

And it continued with the names of Angelo, Nicodemo and Vinicio, which had to be the name of Angelo's sibling. The man was also sitting on a chair, and his legs and arms were tied with thick lengths of rope to it. He wore a dark suit with a special pin attached to it. I couldn't make out what kind of pin it was, though, but if Rita was right about them, then this photo confirmed her suspicions.

They were no common Italian-Americans who ran a restaurant for a living; they were, in reality, members of the Italian mafia.

And now, I worked for them. I didn't gasp and I was thankful for that. I then put the photo back inside the small box. Just underneath it was another picture, and this one brought a wave of warmth to my heart. It was almost as if someone was trying to show me both sides of his life. The photo depicted Angelo and his younger brother. They were standing in front of a soccer field, and Angelo's arm was around his brother's shoulders.

They were smiling so broadly and so truthfully their eyes had narrowed to slits. Both of their cheeks were blushing, and sweat was visible on their skin. They were having fun back then. I flipped the photo again and my eyes read another line of writing.

March 10th, 2004, playing Calcio with dad.

Calcio or soccer, it doesn't really matter, I presumed. *They call it what they want. It's still the same sport.*

Gazing at Angelo in the photograph, who couldn't have been more than fifteen back then, I couldn't help but envision what he would have been like today if his father hadn't become the don of a Mafia family. He had had a bright future ahead of him – one where he didn't have to torture people. But now, things were different, and I wondered if that same kid could ever be brought back?

As I put the photos and all the things that came out of the box back inside it, I wondered if he ever thought about what his life was like when he didn't have to kill and rob people. *Well, it's not my concern*, I concluded as I put the box back on top of his dresser. *I'm nothing more than a waitress here, after all.* I had just grabbed my broom and was going to leave when, unexpectedly, the door opened. In stepped none other than Angelo, whose eyes broadened when they landed on me.

I could almost read his mind asking what the fuck I was doing here before he realized why. In a blink, they went back to their cold, unnerving light as he approached me. I cleared my throat and, as uncomfortableness tainted my tongue, I spoke, "I'm here to clean up your room, sir. Fantino asked me to do it."

His eyes cleared up some more. "Ah, no problem. I guess it required some tidying up." An unsettling moment of silence. "Thanks."

I nodded and walked out of there as quickly as possible without making so obvious for him. The last thing I had wanted was to have him walk into the room while I was still tidying it up.

But of course, it had to happen, and all things considered, I was lucky my presence there hadn't bothered him. He closed the door, and I padded down to the ground floor. The stars were shining faintly in the sky, like they were ashamed of themselves. I then changed to my everyday clothes and grabbed my purse to head back home. A lot transpired today, and I learned so much about him. And Rita needed to know about it all.

CHAPTER 4

A Warning

Alide

She paced in front of me, her hand reaching for her cigarette pack. She drew one out and kindled it using the stove's flame. Her eyes were a painting of concern as she blurted, "You shouldn't continue to work there. It's not safe. I told you about those people. I knew they were Mafia."

"How could you have known?" I shook my head. "Forget it. It doesn't matter."

Her eyes bulged. "It doesn't matter? Are you sure? What if another gang comes shooting the whole place up when you are working there? Do you want Luca to lose his only family?!"

I shook my head again, her words aching my heart. "It's not going to happen. And what do you expect me to do? I can't quit that job. I need the money for us and Luca's medicine."

She threw her arms over her head in frustration and opened her mouth, but it was Luca who then spoke, "What's going on? Why are you two fighting?" He was just outside his room, his hands on the doorway's frame. I hurried to him and went on one knee. "We are not fighting. Don't worry about it." He beheld me with a clear expression of vagueness. Luca had his condition and he was a depressed boy most of the time, but he wasn't stupid. His scores spoke for themselves.

Rita and I just shouldn't have been arguing inside the house.

As the moment of silence thickened, I spoke, "Come on. Back to bed. You'll have a full day tomorrow morning at school."

Luca didn't say anything; he merely gazed at me like he wished he could tell me he didn't believe my words. It made me feel bad, but I still stood up and took him back to bed. I pulled the blanket up to his chin, and turned off the light. I then leaned on the wall of his bedroom and respired. Rita walked over to me, her hand still holding her stinking cigarette. "Just think this through. If something bad happens while you are working there, don't hesitate to quit the job. I'm sure we can find something better for you."

"Thanks," I said, smiling reticently. She padded to the backyard of the house, but I didn't believe we could find another job for me easily. Being accepted to work as a waitress in the Bello Italiano had already been hard enough, after all. *Whatever has to happen*, I was thinking, *I'm going to do the best for Luca.*

Angelo

People walked here and there. Cars and trucks came and went on the road in front of me. I was sitting at a table, alone, and my hands were holding a newspaper. On the table made of iron was a cup of hot tea. My mind was barely aware of the cloudy sky and the birds as they flew from one building to the other, hunting for food.

I flipped one page, and then another, and another until I stumbled upon a title that caught my attention. I was looking, in reality, for the international sports section of the newspaper, but I also couldn't deny that the story they included here mattered to me.

And it counted maybe a bit too much. As I read the title, it was as if the world around me had frozen. *Infertile man finally does it! His wife is so happy she can't believe it!* The title was a bit melodramatic and ridiculous, but it still made me care about the story, and so, I read on. *Dustin Walters has been infertile his whole life. Well, not anymore! Thanks to an intensive treatment and many nights in the operation room, now he can finally have proper sex with his wife, who herself is so happy she can't help but plan a world-wide trip once their baby is born.*

Okay, that got even more ridiculous, but I continued to read on. What kind of harsh therapy did he subject himself to in order to mitigate his infertility?

In our clinics, you can pay for the same treatment Mr. Walters has gone through. If you are a man with the same problem, don't hesitate to call us. Mr. Walters is now happier than ever, and his wife is jubilant to have their first baby. It's all a question of perseverance and believing that it can happen!

It read more like a joke article, and it made me question the truthfulness of it. I pulled out my phone and Googled the name of the clinic.

But the search engine found nothing, like it didn't even exist. This local newsprint had to have been desperate as fuck to have included a piece of fake news like this on one of its pages, I speculated before putting it on the table.

Still, the story made me question if *it* was conceivable. My whole life had been plagued by this fear that I could never make a woman happy without being able to make her pregnant. I tried it many times with Tiziana – that had been my way to make father give up on his quest to make me marry Alide – but it just never worked. I could produce sperm like any man, but it was more translucent than what I had seen in photos on the internet. I didn't think there was a way to fix something like that, and if I ever got a woman pregnant, it would be through sheer luck...

Alide

Checking the calendar, I couldn't help but notice a month had passed since I began to work in the Bello Italiano. Work was tough. It tired me every day, both mentally and physically, but it was still the best option I had. Plus, Mr. Romani treated me so well. It was like he was trying to be a father figure to me or something. I wondered why he took such a liking to me, considering he was the Don of a mafia family.

Well, maybe the Mafia thing was behind them now and they focused only on their restaurant business these last few years. I couldn't know that for sure, but since Rita ceased getting all worked up about me still working here, I kind of pushed aside the memory of that horrible photo which depicted them torturing a man in a suit. I glanced around the room for the customers and padded to Mr. Romani's office. I knocked on his door and then heard him saying, "Come on in, Alide."

I opened the door and gave him a shy smirk. He added, "You've been working here for so long I already know when it's you who's knocking."

"Well, I hope I haven't disappointed, sir," I said, interlacing my hands in front of me in a protective manner. Despite his overall gentleness with me, I still couldn't ignore he was the Don of his Mafia family.

"You have actually exceeded my expectations." He gesticulated with his hand downward. "Sit. I'm going to get your payment."

He opened a drawer and took out of it a couple of money stacks. Just a glance was enough to tell me something was wrong about them. "Here it is," he said, handing them to me. To make sure I wasn't about to tell him something stupid, I counted all the money. He said nothing as I did so. I postulated he was going to say I didn't trust him or something of the sort, which would make me nervous.

Regardless, I still needed to find out if the amount was correct.

But it wasn't. The salary was supposed to be 2880 dollars, but the money stacks amounted to 3500 dollars.

Did something happen? Why was he paying me more than what we agreed on when I signed the contract? And, as far as I knew, he mentioned nothing about bonuses, and I did no extra time, other than that evening when I tidied up his son's room.

"Mr. Romani, I think there's something wrong. You are paying me more than my wage."

He waved his hand in front of him and leaned on the chair. "It's fine. I don't need the extra money. You, on the other hand, do."

I studied his eyes, asking myself if he knew about Luca and how we lived. Did he? Did Angelo tell him something about that? Should he even care, if he was aware? I considered objecting to him paying me more than I needed, but decided not to. He was right. I needed his money, and the extra was enough to save up a big chunk for the PS4 Luca wanted so much.

I could just imagine him jumping around when I told him the good news.

"But Mr. Romani, I don't even know how to thank you."

He stood up and walked with me to the door. "No need to thank me. You are a good girl, and you deserve only the best." I stepped out of his office, my heart still galloping. Rita was going to have to eat her words about Mr. Romani.

"Tell me." His expression grew serious. "What do you think of my son?"

My heart lunged. "Angelo? I... don't know. We haven't spoken much."

"Still, tell me what you think about him. I'm curious."

Why was he curious about that? I had nothing to do with Angelo, even if I thought he was handsome and I wondered if we had a chance together if he was from a different family.

"He's a nice guy, Mr. Romani. He's just like you."

He nodded a couple of times, ruminating my words. "I see. Thank you for speaking your mind." He then smiled. "Well, spend your money wisely. I'll see you back here next week."

"Thank you, Mr. Romani." I bowed. "I won't waste the money, that I promise."

His smile widened a bit, and he then closed the door.

How weird, I asserted it all was as I changed back to my white top and jeans. But hey, if he was willing to pay me more than what I was owed, then what did I have to complain about, right?

CHAPTER 5

Things are Looking Up

Alide

Before going back home, I stopped by the pharmacy and bought Luca's medicine for his coughs. I was so glad I had more than enough money for it. We survived through so many months where we made just the sufficient to put food on the table. It was also going to be nice digesting something that wasn't the local Burger King's menu, I conjectured before getting out of the bus and walking back home.

Maybe, after buying his PS4, I could save enough to send him to a good clinic. We needed to find out why he'd been coughing every day. He didn't always cough blood, but it still happened, and it was reason enough to make me worry about him.

More than ever before, I wished we had a public health care system here in New York. I opened the door to our home and trod in. Luca was sleeping on the couch, making me put my hands on my waist. Rita was sitting on her comfy chair, and the TV was on. I didn't need to glance at it to know what show she was watching.

Westworld.

Her head turned to me, and sensing my disenchantment, she said, "I-I-I wa-was just about to put him on his bed."

"Riiiiight," I said, smirking funnily at her. I sat by Luca, and couldn't help but notice how frail he appeared to be.

His phone was on the floor and the screen had been turned off, I perceived with a glance.

"I've got good news, Rita, and you are going to have to take your words back about Mr. Romani."

Her eyes narrowed as Luca stirred, but didn't wake up. "What do you mean?"

I fished out the money stacks he gave to me, and showed it to her. Her eyes shot open. Despite the shock I knew she was going to have, my mind was thinking about something else.

Couldn't Mr. Romani have paid me through a bank transference? And that's when it hit me.

He couldn't.

As a Don of the Mafia, he couldn't use the bank system like everybody else without compromising his operations. His tendency to be old school made sense to me now.

"Holy shit! That's a lot of money."

"It's 3500 dollars." I fished out the packs with Luca's medicine. "And, I've got these as well."

This time, Luca stirred and fluttered his eyelids open. He sat up on the couch slowly, rubbed his eyes, and glanced at me and Rita. "What's going?" He asked.

I opened a medicine pack and gave him a pill. His eyes widened. "It's for your coughing, Luca. Take it."

He strode to the kitchen, poured some water into a glass, and took it. Upon getting back, I voiced, "Take one in the morning and one at night, okay? It should help you."

He nodded and sat on the couch gently. For the first time that night, his eyes landed on the money stacks, and they shot open. Even someone almost fully blind would have known that was much more money than NYC's minimum wage.

"Holy shit!" He said a bit louder than normal.

I picked up a stack of money and uttered, "This I'm saving up for your PS4."

"For real?"

I nodded. "For real," I responded and hugged him before kissing one of the temples of his head.

He felt so cold.

I wished I could save up the money to send him to a good clinic instead, but I did promise I would buy him a PS4. I couldn't go back on my word like that.

We then all hugged each other as we watched another episode of Westworld. It was horrible, but being with them like this, together and united, more than made up for it.

Angelo

I paced in front of my dad, his nostrils blazing. "I'm not going to keep doing this! She already told me where she last saw him, and it didn't help us." I paused, staring at him. "It's over, father. She can't tell us anything more." He waved his hand in front of him superficially. "Fine, fine. Get her out of there before I change my mind."

I walked to the door as fast as my legs could take me, feeling a surge of annoyance in my heart. Father could be so stubborn when he wanted to. When I wrapped my fingers around the knob, he said, "Did you talk to Alide already? She's been working with us for quite a while now."

"I'm not going over to her to tell her we are going to marry. She doesn't even know what she is to us. Why don't you tell her everything instead?"

"It should be *you*."

"Why should it be me?! I don't want to have to marry her. She would add nothing to our family."

"Enough!" He punched his desk. "You are going to do as I ask of you, and you are not going to spout your bullshit again."

When I threw the door open, he barked, "And her father's vow *will be respected*."

I said nothing. I just closed the door behind me with force and stormed out of there as I ignored Prudenzio's pleas to hear him out about something I didn't care about at all right now. I didn't want to and didn't have the right mind to talk to him about anything at this moment.

And there was still Vinicio. I just hoped he would get out of the city somehow. I was already tired of hunting him down and obeying our father all the time.

Alide

The customers stood up and walked away. *Man, what a mess they left behind.* I pulled out a clean handkerchief and began to clean off the pieces of lasagna that were on the table, putting them on a dustpan. I didn't complain about working here much, but when I did, it was because of something that pissed me off *so. fucking. much.*

Being a waitress here could be so much better if the customers respected me and the other workers. People peregrinated on the sidewalk in front of the restaurant, some with their arms linked. Some were smiling, others were laughing, and some were all alone. The sky wasn't overcast like in most days. The surrounding environment was also being decorated by the sounds of cars driving, accelerating and pulling over. If there was one thing Little Italy should be proud of, it was how it tended to attract many and all kinds of people to it.

I finished putting the pieces of lasagna into a small plastic bag when the front door opened loudly. In stepped Angelo, and for the first time since we met in Central Park that day, he was smiling and laughing as if he had nothing to worry about. I knew it wasn't the case, but that's the impression I got from him.

The customers in the restaurant stopped what they were doing to watch Angelo and his men sitting at one of the tables. I glanced around and found out I was the one supposed to take their orders. My heart raced a little, but I reminded myself I was their waitress and my job was to serve them, regardless of who the customer happened to be. I adjusted my shirt to make sure it looked perfect on me, and then walked to them with my small notepad and four menus in my hands.

There were four of them, including Angelo. I recognized one of the other three. His name was Prudenzio, and if I remembered correctly, he was his right-hand man. I was sure they had a proper title for him in Italian, but I couldn't remember what it was. It mattered nothing to me anyway, and so, I continued to them. They were still laughing and talking noisily about something I couldn't make out, and couldn't care much about. Or maybe, I did care, because I caught myself listening to their words and trying to discern what they were finding so funny.

I also couldn't get my eyes off Angelo.

I couldn't remember have ever seen him looking this happy before. I guessed there were many things about him I still didn't know, and now, more than ever, I wished I could know what they were.

"And then, she farted!" Prudenzio blurted out, making all his friends burst out laughing so hard the other customers stopped what they were doing, again, to glance at them with arbitrating eyes.

I cleared my throat and said as I tried not to sound too judgmental, "Can I help you guys?"

They glanced at each other, and then cleared their throats and adjusted their postures. "We'll have a bacon pizza. Make it large, and get some Budweisers for us as well," Angelo said, sounding more serious and contained this time.

I scribbled their orders and padded out of there. They resumed their chatter, but contained themselves. There was still the occasional laugh or loud sentence, but nothing more than that. The restaurant had returned to its regular level of noise. I stood behind a short wall where the cooks had been making the pizzas. I had just delivered the orders to the main cook, and he said it would take them no time to make them. We also had plenty of Budweiser cans in the main fridge, so that was a nonissue.

And that all meant I had some minutes to think and contemplate... I rested my forearms on the short wall made of red stones and leaned down on it, my body weighing on the structure. It separated the huge fireplace where the pizzas were being baked from the rest of the Bello Italiano.

I sighed and gazed at Angelo. He still smiled and threw his arms over his head whenever he said something I was sure had sounded ridiculous to his friends. They were still cracking jokes, and he was having a good time with them. Seeing him like that made me think, again, that I knew nothing about him... That's when, all of a sudden, he snapped his head to me much before I could look away. Our eyes locked, despite the distance between us. There was something about his gaze which made me feel unpleasant, and something else that I couldn't quite put my finger on.

The stare lasted a couple more seconds until Prudenzio nudged his shoulder and he was then absorbed by their conversation again. By far, they were still the liveliest group in the Bello Italiano. Minutes passed as I checked some messages on my phone and talked to Rita. One of the cooks placed the pizza in front of me, and Fantino helped me with the beer cans. I walked with him to their table, put the pizza down in front of them, and then padded out of there after saying, "*Buon appetito.*"

Fantino strolled with me and commented, "I saw how you were looking at him."

His words startled me, and he must have noticed my reaction, because he smiled in an instant. "Don't worry. I'm not going to tell anyone. I guess it's normal for someone like you to have a crush on him." He approached his head to mine and whispered, "Just don't think he can ever love you back. You know what he's like."

I nodded and said, "Guess so..."

New clients then poured into the establishment, and we proceeded to serve them.

Despite being occupied with their pasta orders and Fantino's words, I couldn't help but steal more glances at Angelo. He was just so handsome, and as he continued to have fun with his friends, he felt more approachable – more human. Before now, I had thought he was the kind of man who could only be uptight and serious all the time. Seeing him having fun made me wish I could have a chance with him, even if that had nothing more than a very slim chance of happening.

And what about *that* stare of his?

Did he like me too?

Why did he stare at me for so long until his best friend had to nudge him? Questions and more questions, but only one stood out.

We don't really choose who we love, do we?

CHAPTER 6

Betrayal

Angelo

I closed the front door as my friends left the restaurant. They were my soldiers, foremost, but I still thought of them as my friends. Father didn't like that much, but hey, what could he do about it? People were beginning to leave the restaurant now, and the lights poles had been turned on outside. Behind the buildings, I could see the sun as it set. Fewer cars were going down and up the road in front of the establishment.

Another day was passing by, and I still hadn't talked to Alide about who she was and our supposed marriage. Doing that would be akin to committing myself to a wedding I still didn't want to make happen, and I would like to avoid it for as long as possible.

Maybe a couple of months from now father would change his mind... I glanced to one side and found *her*. Alide was chatting with one of the waiters, and her cheeks were blushing. Her eyes looked so lively and full of energy. She was having fun, and that was good. I didn't want to marry her, but if she managed to find someone right for her, then why not let it happen? Father wouldn't then be able to do much about anything, unless he wanted to tell her what she should know himself.

She had quite the hair, the cheeks and lips. She was stunning, and even more gorgeous than Tiziana, and that was saying something.

Her body, despite the waitress uniform, looked perfect, and made me wish I could have her in my arms.

And then... maybe on my bed too.

I shook the thought away. Daydreaming about her appearance would do me no good. As I walked back to my father's office to talk to him about Vinicio and another lead I might have on him, I reminisced about the stare we had had. It was like I had been feeling someone was watching me from a distance, and upon having snapped my head in her direction, I had discovered I hadn't been hallucinating after all. Alide had indeed been watching me, and something in her eyes had told me she shared some of my feelings for her.

But even if she did, did that even matter? It was not like we could ever work. She was too different. She wouldn't merge well in a world like mine. I killed and made people suffer. She was far too sweet, in contrast.

And if she wanted a kid of our own, short of adopting one, I wouldn't be able to provide it to her. *Damn being infertile*, I cursed before opening the door without knocking on it first. Father didn't need me to knock to know it was me who was coming in. His eyesight was pretty bad, but his hearing more than made up for it, after all.

"Father, I've got another lead on Vinicio, but I don't think you are going to like it."

He frowned his forehead. "Speak, my son. I don't have time to waste."

"He's with the Ancelottis now. For some reason, they think he can be of help to them."

He punched his stable and stood up in a flash. "Of course that traitor can be of help to them. He knows too much." A moment of pause as he paced behind the desk. "You are going to have to get to him somehow. Use as many men as you need. *Don't let him talk.*"

I nodded, and just when I was about to leave, he probed, "Have you spoken with Alide already?"

I sighed. "No, I haven't yet."

"God fucking dammit, Angelo. I thought I'd raised you better."

"I'll... talk to her soon."

I closed the door. *Soon* was actually going to take a long while. *As long as needed until my old man was dead*, I reaffirmed before finding Prudenzio as he smoked a cigarette in front of the building.

I gestured with my hand for him to follow me. "C'mon on. We need to find Vinicio"

* * *

Prudenzio paced in front of my desk, his hand cupping his chin. He was thinking, as was I. Was there a way to get to my brother without alerting all of the Ancelottis?

That goal seemed unreachable. Vinicio was in their hideout, and it was like a fortress. Men patrolled not only its border, but also the adjacent neighborhoods. Prudenzio shot his finger up straight, and beamed, "I think I've got an idea. Not sure you are going to like it, though."

I sighed and looked at nowhere in particular. "Just say what it is. I'm done playing cat and mouse with him."

He strode to me, his eyes burning with a bright light of lucidity. "You are going to love this."

* * *

We pulled over just outside their defensive perimeter and slipped out of the Chrysler before anyone could catch sight of us. We wore black coats, pants and boots. The combination was perfect for a rainy light like this one. And I was glad it was raining; it was going to make getting to Vinicio much easier. If all went as according to Prudenzio's plan, I wouldn't even have to use my gun. We stopped by an alleyway, the road behind us uninhabited. No citizens were walking on the sidewalk, and no cars were coming or going on the road. The next light pole was a couple of miles away.

Other than the light coming from the windows of the small high-rises, there were no other signs that this part of the town was inhabited, I reflected before peeking my head to find a couple of men talking among themselves in between four buildings. Prudenzio and I had hidden ourselves behind the walls of two high-rises, and our eyes were now studying what those guys were doing.

They were from the Ancelotti family and were going to be my ticket to Vinicio. I didn't plan on taking Prudenzio with me. In case things turned sour, he would go to my father and tell him the bad news. I pulled out my Colt and nodded to Prudenzio.

We studied this through. We'd had no idea we were going to find those men precisely in this location, but it was perfect nonetheless.

The locale was as silent and uninhabited as it could get for New York City, I additionally weighed when we lurched in their direction.

Prudenzio grabbed my arm and whispered, "I'm going to draw them out. You take care of the rest." I nodded, and he prowled toward them. There was a path of sorts connected to the alleyway, and it led all the way to the other side of it. It was perfect for the kind of plan we had in mind.

I waited in the shadows for Prudenzio to show up there. Seconds after he did, he shouted some obscenities to the Ancelottis. They shouted back at him, and some of them picked up their submachine guns and pistols as they chased my best soldier.

I heard their hurried footsteps as they left the premises. I peeked at the end of the alleyway and found, this time, two guys. They had most likely been asked to stay here,

33

since they couldn't leave their post unattended and Prudenzio was just one man. Adding to that, the Ancelottis chasing him at this moment were probably thinking they could get him without breaking a sweat.

I smirked waywardly. They knew nothing about him and his capabilities. I prowled to those men. Their backs were turned to me. One of them babbled, "Idiot is probably dead at this point. Must have been too drunk to care who he was messing with."

The other chuckled and nudged his shoulder. "Hey, at least we don't have to chase anybody tonight."

"Keep your eyes peeled, though. Anything can happen when your guard is down."

"My guard-"

I pulled the trigger, killing the guy that was talking last. His friend stood up in a flash, his hand going for and now holding his submachine gun. I had a silencer with me, so nobody in the vicinity had heard anything, and even if they had, they probably had concluded it had been just a rat running through their ventilation ducts or something of the sort. These men had all been sitting here on cheap plastic chairs, I noticed. The rain still poured, soaking the lower parts of my pants. In this locale, they had some makeshift covers to protect themselves from the rainwater, but it was barely enough for all of them. A minivan stood in the alleyway not too far from where I was, and the raindrops that fell on it were making so much noise I could barely hear the guy when he blurted again.

"Stay back, or I'll shoot!"

Seriously?

That goon gave off the impression he was a danger to himself and not to me. And here I thought all the Ancelottis were hardened soldiers. This one here, whose hand kept shaking as I got soaked by the rain, looked like a pussy.

And he was one.

"Now, let's not do anything rash."

I stepped forward, and a shot exploded in the air, hitting the ground not too far from me.

"Fuck!"

I dashed ahead before he could pull the trigger again, jumped and made him topple over with me.

I was on top of him now, and I then punched his face a couple of times until he couldn't resist me anymore. His hand let go of his submachine gun, showing me I'd won.

I pointed my Colt at his face and spat, "Don't push me again, or you are going to regret it."

He nodded.

And that's how I was going to get to Vinicio.

CHAPTER 7

Tell me the Truth

Angelo

I put on his friend's clothes, which included a black fedora hat, and we marched out of there in the direction of the Ancelottis' hideout. He was reluctant, but with my gun trained at him, he could do nothing but obey me. I asked him about Vinicio. He knew he was with them, and now, he was taking me to him.

What was going to happen from then on... Well, that depended on him.

I also hid his dead friend's body. He expressed nothing about him. That's how the Ancelottis rolled. They didn't care about each other much. The rain had dwindled a little outside, but it was still there. The man whose name I didn't bother to ask opened a door, took me through some security checkpoints where all I had to do was to look confident or hide my face - depending on who was at them - and then stopped in front of a black door with nothing but one guy guarding it.

He murmured to the man about letting me through, and he did so after glancing over my face. I faked that I looked confident to make sure they couldn't recognize my face. Pretending that was true sickened me a little, but it was nothing compared to Vinicio having chosen them of all gangs in the city to partner himself with.

The man guarding the black, battered door crept it open, and I stepped through. Just as I expected, he immediately shut the door and I then found myself all alone with a shorter-than-me, skinny man who was sitting on a couch, watching TV.

His face and torso jerked to me, standing up from the couch an instant later.

I sped to him before he could scream and call everyone to us. I needed this moment of solitary conversation with him, and he wasn't going to ruin that. I pounded him against the wall without making too much noise, and thanks to the rain outside, I knew the Ancelottis in the building hadn't heard anything. His eyes shot wide as I covered his mouth with my hand. He screamed, but the sound came out so muffled it probably didn't penetrate the thick walls of this room.

"Shhhhh! I'm not here to kill you. We need to talk."

I waited until his eyes stopped trembling. When he ungripped my arm, I knew he wasn't going to scream. Vinicio was many things to me, and one of them was that he could trust me whenever he needed to.

I hadn't come here to kill him. That was out of the question. Father asked me to bring him alive, and I didn't want to end the life of my only brother. Just fixating at him now... I couldn't help but remember just how much he meant to me.

"If you are not here to kill me, then what do you want? To talk? We've got nothing to talk about."

"I need you not to tell the Ancelottis about us. If you do, it would be like sending us to our graves."

"I haven't planned on telling them anything. I'm here just for their protection." He stopped for a second, and then continued, "Father abhors me, after all."

"Well, yeah, he does. You did the opposite of what he asked of you."

"I had no choice. He wanted me to kill and rob people. I'm not like *him*."

"The rest, lik-" I was saying the moment I heard hastened footsteps approaching us. Fuck. I knew that guy was going to end up telling his friends what was going on.

I glimpsed at the window at the other end of the room.

That's my escape.

I jerked my finger at his face and promised, "If you tell them anything about us, I'll have no choice but to kill you."

And I didn't wait for his response.

I spun and bolted to the window. I jumped and then broke through it before barrel-rolling on the ground. The door up there was kicked open, and then Ancelottis shouted something about Vinicio staying right where he was right before a couple of them popped at the window. They had assault rifles and machine guns trained at me, but the fog and the rain made it too difficult for them to get a clear shot at me. Regardless, they opened fire.

Before they could think of a better plan to off me, I was already scurrying through the many alleyways and dark roads with only one objective in mind. More than ever before, I needed to make our father change his mind about Vinicio.

Alide

I should have known Fantino was going to ask me to come here to tidy up another room. I leaned on a wall and sighed. *Working here is so hard.*

There were far too many customers complaining about the littlest of things. It was like they came here to whine all the time. It maddened me.

I could only hope I would, one day, make enough to find a better job elsewhere. The only thing that comforted me was Mr. Romani's nicety. He was always gentle with me, like a father would. I recalled that, more than anything, I needed the money for Luca's medicine, and so, I leaned off the wall and minced to the room Fantino had asked me to clean up. I should have asked one of the other waitresses to stay here with me so that I could have begged her to do this thing for me. Outside, the night was serene, though there were still people walking on the sidewalks as they chatted loudly, and some cars were driving on the road as well. It was nothing more than the usual for a night here in Little Italy.

Despite the rumors, I hadn't experienced anything close to a shootout in this neighborhood, and that had reaffirmed my belief that I could continue to work here. I put my hand on the door of the living room when, suddenly, I heard the sound of a shower being turned on somewhere else. Not too long after, steam began to come out through the gap of a door.

The sight piqued my curiosity.

Who was taking a shower at this time of the night?

I knew I was nosy, but did I really have to go there to check it out?

No, of course not.

But I still did. I left the bucket with water and the mop by the entrance of the living room, and sashayed to where the steam was coming from. I put a hand on the doorway – the door was semi-open – and peeked inside.

My heart, which was racing a little, as usual, leaped when my eyes landed on *him*. It was Angelo. He was the one taking a shower, and he was washing his hair with shampoo. I couldn't help but scan his body from bottom to top. He was stunning. Every muscle of his seemed to have been sculpted by God himself.

And he had a happy trail that went from his belly button to his cock.

The steam made it impossible for me to see his private parts, but I still knew – or was just as sure as I could be – that he was hung and hadn't shaved down there in a while. I sighed unhurriedly, thinking about what it would be like if only we could have a chance.

But we hadn't even had a proper conversation yet.

And why should we have had one anyway? He was from a different world.

He had nothing to do with me. With that depressive conclusion in mind, I minced back to where I had been and went to clean the living room. It was good seeing him naked for the first time, but that was that. He was a mafia member, and I was nothing more than the waitress of his father's establishment. I'd do well to keep that in mind.

* * *

It's another day and the restaurant was packed, as usual. I had to go from table to table, taking the customers' orders, deliver them to the cooks, and then come back with their plates, pizzas and drinks. No wonder Mr. Romani had chosen this line of business to build his fortune on. He probably made much more than what I could wrap my head around. I opened a door and walked from the main compartment of the Bello Italiano to the backside of it. That's when my eyes landed on Angelo.

He was at the end of the hallway, chatting with Prudenzio and two of his other soldiers. On his face was a painting of absolute seriousness and attention.

I didn't know what they were talking about, but I still stood there for a couple of seconds, watching Angelo.

Once again, I couldn't help but admire the lines of his face, his mud-colored eyes, and that pitch-black hair. And his stubble... Ahhhh. It was, in my opinion, one of his best features. Everything about him seemed flawless, as if it had all been made to look the way it was, and his excessive self-esteem was like the cherry on top of everything.

He was my type, but I knew I wasn't his.

He'd never paid any att–

But that was when his eyes zapped to me.

They were trained on Prudenzio before, but when he and another soldier started talking about something I couldn't be bothered to remember, that's when he glanced and stared at me.

Just like that time I was serving him and his friends, we'd locked our eyes with each other.

I froze. I didn't know what to do. I knew he was the son of my boss. If he as much as thought I was going to become a nuisance here, he wouldn't hesitate to fire me.

And that's not something I could afford. Luca needed me, after all, and I was his only light.

Prudenzio then suddenly prodded Angelo, and he finally broke the stare. I could almost thank him now, I thought with a sigh.

I sighed out of pure relief, and went on to do what I'd been told to do, which was to ask Mr. Romani how he would like the new Italian flag to be set up in front of the restaurant.

But for a couple of unnerving seconds, I'd thought the stare was going to last forever.

Angelo

For a moment, I'd deduced her gaze was going to eat me alive. Did she know about the marriage thing already? Did my father finally tell her about it?

Doubtful.

Had he done it, she wouldn't still be here working as a waitress.

That meant... Well, I didn't want to think about it that way. Prudenzio then articulated something about drawing Vinicio out of the Ancelottis' hideout somehow, and I listened to him, though half of my brain was now focused on Alide. And I hated myself for that.

Why should I be thinking about her when we had no chance of ever making the marriage happen? And ah, of course. She first needed to be told about it.

It needed to come out of my mouth – that's what father kept insisting on, anyway. It was what he wanted, even if I was stalling for as long as I could. Someone blurted something about a shootout near the Ancelottis' hideout while I still thought about Alide.

She'd looked so gorgeous and angelic, even in her waitress uniform.

There was something about it – maybe it was the lack of makeup – that brought the best out of her. She had no idea what was going on, what father wanted, and I really wanted to keep things that way. That innocent look in her eyes... It was something she wouldn't continue having if she were to learn about his plans for her.

I nodded and shared, "We'll get him out of there."

They all dipped their heads too, showing me they understood what was at stake, and I then sauntered back to my bedroom. I grabbed a book, sat on the bed and began to read it. *Infertility Doesn't Have To Be A Problem.*

Yeah, right. *I need to control this obsession,* I reprimanded myself for still having this book. Nevertheless, pushing that thought to the sidelines for now, it was not like the people who wrote this knew what was going on.

For the most part, it didn't have to be an issue, but after the marriage and if Alide wanted a child of our own, I didn't know if I would have the courage to tell her we just couldn't make it happen. Or I could simply avoid the subject while we kept trying. By then, my father would be dead and Alide would just think we hadn't been having any luck.

Maybe it wouldn't be such a big deal after all...

I closed the book and read the author's name. This guy understood nothing about it, if he even was a dude. So many authors used pen names these days to hide their true identities, after all. I went to the balcony of the restaurant and smoked. As I watched the people down below, the cars, and admired the buildings, I conjectured what the future held in store for Alide here. The sun began to set in the distance, and the customers had started to leave the establishment. Little Italy grew a bit silent and serene as the minutes went by.

Maybe half an hour or an hour had already passed since I opened the book, I thought before tossing the cigarette butt over the balcony and strutting back inside. I took the stairs down to the ground floor and heard a faint sound.

It was of something or someone rustling.

Somebody could be changing clothes, or maybe it was one of the Ancelottis having funny ideas about sneaking in here to kill my father.

I pulled out my Colt and peeked inside the room.

That's when my pupils landed on her. *Alide.*

It was the first time I was seeing her naked like this. Well, not fully naked. She had her bra and panties on, and was in the process of putting on her jeans pants. Still, that was the most of her I had ever seen until this moment, and I couldn't help but feel my cock hardening.

Control yourself, Angelo. She isn't for you.

Yeah, I knew that, but it didn't mean I couldn't contemplate beauty when it was exposed like this. She had curves to make most women envious of her, and she was even more striking than Tiziana. The innocence in her eyes was something I couldn't find easily elsewhere. It was alien, and it should be protected. Problem was, by putting her here and forcing me to approach her, father was ending all that.

She had a hair I had never seen before. It shone brightly under the soft light of the room she was in, and it looked smooth like silk. I knew she was poor and, thus, also probably didn't tend to use many beauty products to keep it that way. And considering she had been working here for eight hours straight today, the quality of her hair was a testament to her natural splendor. I sighed and put my gun back in my waistband. She had just finished putting on her black top and was going to leave the Bello Italiano. I padded out of there without making much noise and before she could realize I'd been spying on her.

No point letting her know I was nearby, I warned myself. She felt so distant, and I just had no chance of making us work.

Father will, one day, just have to understand that.

* * *

I took the stairs and swaggered down to the ground floor. Alide had been working for us for some months now, and dad had been just as persistent as usual about me telling her about the marriage.

He had many other things to occupy his time, like Vinicio and the Ancelottis, and so, he hadn't been pestering me much about the wedding.

Outside, the sun was glowing like a hot spotlight, and the street was teeming with people and all kinds of vehicles. I rounded a corner and was heading to the parking space behind the establishment. I needed to get my car and drive to the bowling alley Prudenzio was. He enunciated to me before he had something important about Vinicio to tell me. *It will make getting him out of there much easier* was what he'd informed me over the phone.

And that was when, abruptly, I picked up her voice. *Alide.*

She was in the kitchen room, talking with someone over the phone. I couldn't see her, but her voice was as clear as day. I could also pick up some scattered words from her friend too.

They mattered nothing to me, though. What was of great importance was learning what Alide herself was beaming about.

I leaned on the wall of the room which helped to compose the hall, and listened.

"Rita, I had no idea you have a boyfriend. I thought you were over dating."

Strangely enough, leaning on the wall and closing my eyes made me capable of making out the words from who I assumed to be her friend. Rita? I could almost be certain I had heard that name before. Maybe my father had mentioned her once months or years ago. Alide didn't have a mom anymore, after all.

"Yeah, I know. But he's getting so fat and is also refusing to get a haircut. I need to do something about him."

"But do what? If he's your boyfriend, then I'm assuming you like him."

"Yeah, I do, but I began dating him partially because he had perfect abs. Seeing him in his current condition is so depressing..."

Alide chuckled. It sounded like the most charming chuckle I had heard in quite a while, and it brought a gentle smirk to my face.

"You know, I don't really care about someone's looks that much. I mean, it matters for an initial attraction, but after that, I want something more substantial, but that's just my opinion."

"Alide, stop with that bullshit. You are making me cry. I don't want to give up on him. It's just that..." She stopped for a moment. "I can't go out anymore with my friends without them making fun of me."

Alide chuckled again, and it sounded just as adorable as the first time. "Forget about them. I'm the only friend you need."

"You are right. You are a precious jewel, and I don't know what I'd been doing right now without you."

Alide chuckled adorably again. "Look, Rita. Just speak with him. Tell him what's bothering you. If he likes you that much, he will listen and change."

A moment of silence as Rita digested her friend's advice.

"Alright, Alide. Thanks. I'll do that."

"And just for the record, I also don't really care about things people can't control. Some people are born with problems they can do nothing about. It's okay. We all have things we wished we could change."

There was a long, audible side on the other side of the phone. "You are right, Alide. You are a good girl. I need to go now. I'll see you tonight."

"Okay, see ya."

They completed the call, which meant I needed to resume heading to the parking space behind the Bello Italiano.

Huh. I hadn't thought, when I halted by the wall, that I was going to hear Alide babbling about how problems people could do nothing about didn't bother her. I knew the connection was silly, but I thought back to my infertility. It was something I could do nothing about, and I had been doing a lot of research on the subject, so I knew my conclusion was most likely the right one.

If only I weren't sterile... It was the only thing about myself that cracked my confidence. If father or Tiziana were to find out I couldn't make a woman pregnant... Well, let's just say the outcome wouldn't be nice.

Still, it was reassuring to know Alide would probably not be bothered by that. Maybe marrying her wouldn't be such a bad thing after all.

CHAPTER 8

Shattering False Perceptions

Alide

I checked the time on my phone. Six in the morning. Wow, I got here way too early, I thought before opening the front door. I didn't need the key. It was already open. Maybe Fantino had already arrived and was changing to his work attire.

If he were here, then I couldn't wait to chat with him.

I had something very crucial and good to tell him. I had finally saved up enough money to buy a PS4 for Luca! But that's when my ears picked up a discussion. It was heated, fiery. Two men were as if they were going to rip each other's throat out with their bare hands. I froze where I stood, not knowing if I should proceed or take a stroll in Times Square to kill some time until it was 6:30.

I shook my head and thought there was no point in wasting time. It would be good to do some things beforehand to make the day feel less convoluted.

I couldn't help but notice how their heated discussion was the only thing cracking the otherwise serene atmosphere in Little Italy. Everyone else was either napping or having breakfast right now, I considered, though I quickly shoved the thought away. No point thinking about something like that at this moment.

I walked to the small changing room they had by the kitchen when I recognized who was discussing with you.

It was Mr. Romani and his son, and I was now close enough to make out their words.

"It's been months and you still haven't told her anything."

"You are not making this easier on me!"

"I should have known you were a pussy."

What the fuck were they arguing about?

"Forget it. I'm leaving now."

"No, you are not."

I heard a loud thud, which probably came from Mr. Romani slamming the door closed.

Witnessing him so pissed off like that made me afraid of him. Of course he could be like that. He was the Don of his mafia family, after all.

I shouldn't have let his excessive gentleness make me think highly of him. He probably killed many people and committed so many other crimes I most likely couldn't even imagine how many they were.

"You need to tell her about the marriage. She can't continue to be left in the limbo like that."

"I'll do it, father, when the time's right."

"And when will that be? I thought I had raised you better. You are just stalling."

"I'm not. It's just not easy. Nothing of this is."

An arranged wedding? I wondered who he was going to marry.

And... there went any chance I had of ever getting as much as a date with him. Internally, I cried. *I should have known his father had already chosen the woman that will marry him.* That's how the Mafia operated, after all.

"Well, then stop being a coward and just tell her, or else I'm going to have to do it myself."

A moment of silence, and then, Angelo spoke, "About Vinicio..."

"Tell me you know a way to get him out of there."

"I do, and it will work. Don't worry about it. I'll bring him back."

"You better do. I'm not in the habit of letting the Ancelottis think they got me with my pants down. They are going to *regret* what they did."

"Father, I spoke to him. Vinicio is frightened. He swore he's not telling the Ancelottis anything about us. He still cares about the family."

"Like hell he does! He's nothing more than a traitor, and when I get my hands on h-"

"Please, just let us first get him out of there, and then we can decide what to do with him."

"Why? You think you can convince me he's not a rat? If it's not the Ancelottis he's consorting with, then it will be the feds, and I can't risk the wellbeing of our family more than it already is."

Vinicio? I remembered that name...

So, he's hunting down his own brother? An immense wave of pity for him flooded my heart. I had no idea he was being forced to do something like that.

I thought back to Luca. I would never be able to lay a finger on him, much less chase him with a gun in my hand

"Nothing, father." Angelo lamented. "I'm going now."

Silence, and then, the door crept open. I finally moved and strode away to the changing room by the kitchen. But when I crossed the hallway, I almost collided against him. It was a good thing he dodged me at the last second. Fire and ice stormed in his eyes at the same time. He examined me for a second, and I evaluated I could see something different about his stare, as if there was a problem consuming his mind.

Maybe it was his brother? I could only guess what was going on in a mind like his.

"Sorry, Alide." He stepped aside and continued, "Good to see you here again."

Those sentences were already more than what we spoke to each other in months. And I couldn't help but love the tone and intensity of his voice.

Despite having just had a heated discussion with his father, he managed to recompose himself in a matter of seconds. The front door opened and closed. His father was inside his office room, and I could hear the sound of a pen writing on paper.

He was working. On what, I had no idea, but it had to be something related to his Mafia business.

I wondered, though, what woman Angelo was going to marry, and why he felt so reluctant to tell her the truth. I kind of felt some pity for him.

It was clear as day his arranged wedding was consuming him from the inside out, after all...

Angelo

I pulled over and got out of the car. I checked my Colt. It was there, loaded and ready. I needed to talk to this man – John – about getting some guns. We were planning a shootout outside the Ancelottis' dominated neighborhood to draw most of them out. During the confusion, I would snatch Vinicio out of there and convince father not to hurt him.

That was my strategy. Lower Manhattan was teeming with people and cars, as usual. The sky wasn't overcast, but it had enough cumulus clouds to block a good portion of the sunlight. I had to dodge and zig-zag my way through the many people on the sidewalk.

For the first time in my life, I wished John lived somewhere less crowded. *Better to hide in plain sight*, I could almost hear him reprimanding me.

I circumnavigated a corner and stopped dead.

A man grunted and complained about me being in his way, but I paid no attention to him. I had seen her. *Alide.*

It was Sunday, so she didn't have to work. She was as attractive as ever, with a red top and usual pair of jeans.

She was in front of the GameStop store, and her hand was holding a little boy's. He couldn't be more than 10, and he was crying.

His tears, however, weren't out of sadness. That was as clear as this sunny day to me.

This was most likely the gladdest day of his life. She pointed at the store and the two walked in. I finally relaxed and shuffled to the store. I didn't have to be doing this, but I was.

John's apartment was on the other side of the road, but I felt compelled not to go there and, instead, stalk them.

I halted in front of the store. The panels were made of transparent glass, and despite how crowded this GameStop was, I could still see her.

Alide and the boy were in front of a shelf with several PS4 boxes. She was pointing at them, and I wished I could make out what she was saying.

I wished I could hear her gentle and tender voice again...

A woman smacked against me, but remained where I was. It was as if the world around me didn't matter at all.

Alide picked up one of the blue PS4 boxes, and the little boy smiled so broadly I thought he would never smile like that again in his life. They both turned and headed to the desk. I spun and hid behind the alleyway by the building. Some minutes later, Alide and the young boy got out of the store. They stopped in front of it, and now I could finally make out their words.

The young boy was the first to speak, "I can't believe I finally have it! Thank you so much, big sis!"

Big sis? He was her brother?

I had no idea she had one. I inched my head past the edge of the wall I was hiding behind at, and peeked at them. Alide had bent down and was hugging her little brother.

She was crying. Witnessing them like that warmed my heart. There was still hope for this world. In her hands was a white plastic bag with the PS4 box in it, and when they turned to leave, the boy coughed.

Blood came out in beads. Despite not knowing him, I worried. Was he ill? Was there something I could do to help her?

Would she be okay with that?

She got on one knee, much to the displeasure of a hurried businessman who grunted as he barked on his phone. "I'm going to need to save up money to send you to a clinic. Your coughing has been going for far too long."

The boy's head lowered. "Okay. I know."

She ruffled his hair. "It's not your fault."

And with that said, she grabbed his hand and led him out of there. I leaned back on the wall and looked at nowhere in particular. I didn't think she had a little brother – like I did – and had been saving up money to buy him a console.

Jesus, and here I was thinking my problems were unfair.

She could be naïve to my style of life, what it was like, but there was no denying she knew pain too.

I reckoned Alide was carefree – at work, she always seemed like that. But she understood what it was like to feel pain, hardships, and to battle through them.

They were just different adversities, but in the end, maybe she wasn't so different from my world after all.

And about her younger sibling... What did he have?

* * *

Outside, there was nothing more than a dense fog in Little Italy. I couldn't see more than a couple of meters in front of me. I leaned off the balcony and walked back inside my bedroom. It was neatly kept, and there was nothing scattered on the floor.

The maid father had *finally* hired was doing her job well. I opened the door and walked out. It was night outside. The street was as silent as it could get in a nighttime in New York city. There were the occasional honking and plane flying overhead, but other than that, I could almost feel like I was all alone. I padded to the ground floor, and my ears picked up the sound of someone weeping and crying.

I didn't panic.

It appeared to be a woman. Maybe it was one of the maids. They usually stayed late after their shift to finish some stuff up, after all.

We paid them extra whenever that happened, so it was a nonissue.

But that tone... I thought I knew it. I crept to where the crying was coming from, and inched my head past the wall. My eyes landed on none other than *Alide*. She was all alone. She was sitting on a chair, using her white napkin to wipe her tears. Witnessing her like that broke my heart.

Her whole face was red, like she was frustrated with something. Should I go there? Should I talk to her?

The query of the century it was.

She still felt so distant now, like there was a whole void between us. That's when she lifted her head, and her eyes landed on me. Well, now I had no choice but to approach her. My whole body felt like it was made of rock. I cleared my throat and shuffled to her. Despite not making much noise as I walked, it felt like I was stepping on eggshells.

"I'm sorry, sir. I shouldn't be crying on the job," she vocalized, breaking my heart even more. She sniffed twice, and it was then I knew I couldn't escape her. I thought she was carefree, but seeing her like this and having witnessed her with her brother before, I knew I was wrong. I had been wrong about her this whole time.

She's a woman who knew agony.

And we connected in more ways than I thought possible.

"There's nothing to be sorry about. We are all allowed to cry every once in a while."

I opened a comfortable smile, drawing her eyes to me. She chuckled and stated, "No need to sugar coat it for me. It won't happen again, I promise."

I knew why she was talking like this to me now. She was worried she was going to lose her job. If there was something wrong about her younger brother, like some kind of illness that couldn't be cured, she needed money for his medicine.

And, bearing in mind how much she loved him, also more money for his PS4's games. She stood up in a flash and was saying how sorry she was about all this when I grabbed both of her wrists. Her eyes locked with mine, and they were permeated with red veins. The skin around them had been brushed by a tone of red mixed with purple.

What was making her feel this much pain?

I let go of her wrists, which then fell to the sides of her body. All I needed was to talk to her.

"Alide, I know I'm not your friend or anything, but if there's someone or something here bothering you, just tell me. I can teach him a lesson he will never forget."

She sniffed, and her cheeks had been painted by the lines of her tears. She didn't deserve what was making her so depressed.

Alide shook her head.

"It was nothing, really. I have these breakdowns sometimes, but they always pass."

She smiled, but I knew it was fake. There was a speck of dust on her cheek. I inched my hand up to it, and she noticed it. I continued inching it, slowly and carefully. The last thing I needed was to make her feel more scared than she was. I brushed the speck of dirt off her face and said, "If there's anything you need of me, don't hesitate to ask. I might not be your friend, but I'm still here to help."

Alide grinned and said, "It's okay. It's a deal, but right now, I just need to get back home."

She hurried to the door, but I put an arm in front of her. I knew what still was going on in her mind. She was so apprehensive I was going to tell my father about this. But I wasn't.

"Want a ride back home? Like on your first day here?" I offered.

She seemed like she didn't know what to do with her hand. I knew she was distraught, but I didn't envision my offer was going to have such an effect on her. At long last, she smiled, and despite the sadness that tainted it, it was beautiful and white like a wedding dress.

"Yes, sir. I would like that."

A moment of silence as I cherished her beautifulness, yet sad face some more. She was the kind of woman who hid so much and didn't share it with anyone, other than her friend, Rita. Her eyes gleamed under the fluorescent light of the kitchen, and they were the perfect representation of the past that molded Alide. Despite all the shit she went through, including the passing of her father, she was still a citizen willing to battle all obstacles that dared to stand in her way. And now, more than anything, I venerated that of her.

* * *

She changed back to her everyday clothes and hopped inside my car, as if nothing had happened. Her face was sporting a gentle smirk. It was like Alide had nothing that could worry her. Despite how hard she was trying to keep it hidden, it was evident, though, how much she wanted to make me think she wasn't going to be an issue.

If only I could tell her not to be concerned about that.

But I couldn't.

We didn't have the intimacy for something like that, and I was taking her home – nothing more than that. I couldn't deny, however, that getting to know more about her life made her more reachable to me. Maybe I could make the marriage work then, though there was still the question of her wanting a baby and me being infertile.

Most of all, I didn't want to disappoint my future wife, even if she didn't know her father vowed to make her marry me. I still remembered that stormy night, when I was a teenager and he and dad had signed that agreement...

I began to drive her through lower Manhattan, following the roads to Brooklyn. During the first few minutes, she didn't speak, but when the Brooklyn bridge was within viewing distance, she finally did.

"I'm still so sorry you had to see me like that in your kitchen, Mr. Angelo. It won't happen again."

Despite being aware of the possible repercussions of revealing this, I declared, "It's okay to cry. I do too, from time to time."

I smirked and turned to face her. Her expression was one of surprise mixed with alarm.

Alide then nudged my shoulder and said, joy in her tone, "You? Crying? You don't need to lie to me to make me feel better. See? I already do."

She jutted her chin and looked ahead, like she wanted so hard to guarantee she wasn't lying. But that still present redness in her eyes... It made me sure her past and current life were still bothering her. I wished I could know her full story, and I kind of blamed dad right now for not taking better care of them. I smirked gently as we crossed the Brooklyn bridge and continued to make our way to her home. She was better now, more jovial, but still a bit bothered by what made her cry.

A wild thought crossed my mind. Should I make this one question that's nagging me?

I cleared up my mind, and the answer was a solid NO – for now, at least.

I pulled over by her house. I knew where it was since coming here that one time. It was strange how I could remember the exact address after having come here just once.

Maybe Alide detected that as well, but she made no comments on it. She opened the passenger's door and turned her head to me. She grinned, looking as gorgeous as ever. I also couldn't help but notice how her eyes and her whole face looked better now. What depressed and angered her back in the kitchen was gone, for the most part.

"Thanks for taking me here," she observed, her voice jovial once more. She was going back to being her normal, carefree self.

Just when she was going to close the door, I inquired, "How about a ride back home every day?"

Alide blinked twice, her grin fading. "Oh, you don't need to do that. I'm fine with taking the bus."

Once again, she didn't know what to do with her hands. "It's okay. It wouldn't be a bother to me."

She opened her mouth, but reconsidered her words. "It's a deal, then. From tomorrow on, I'll have my knight to bring me back home every evening." I smirked softly and she closed the door. As I drove back to the Bello Italiano, I couldn't help but feel happy about the outcome of this.

Things were progressing well, and I just had my first normal conversation with her. Truth was, now that I knew more about her, I grew more confident and assured about our wedding. And maybe, soon, I was going to tell her about it. That, though, still stood like a sky-high mountain to climb. *Better to keep taking baby steps for now.*

Alide

I heard a couple of gunshots in the distance, but thought little about them. Rita was sleeping in her bedroom, her snores audible even here in the living room.

Luca was sitting on the couch, and his fingers were playing with the controller of his PS4. He couldn't stop playing it. I even had to control him sometimes so that he didn't slack off on his homework.

That's when, all of a sudden, I heard a loud knock outside. Someone then grunted. I snapped my head to Luca, who was still so worried about that horde of Locusts he needed to exterminate in Gears of War he couldn't blink. My heart leaped when I heard the man grunting again. I took one last look at Luca, and bolted to the door. If there was someone in pain in the front yard, then I needed to do something. Help him or call the ambulance. Whatever he needed and I could do, I was going to.

I threw the door open and my eyes landed on none other than Angelo. He was on the grass, clutching his belly. I ran up to him, and his eyes darted to me. He had been grunting up until that point.

Upon noticing I was coming, he stopped doing that, though it was evident he wasn't lying about having been hurt.

I got on my knees beside him in a wink and asked, "Did something happen? Why are you here?"

Slowly, he sat up on the grass and smirked. "I was chasing this bastard when he hid behind your wall and kicked me in the stomach. Fucking lunatic will get what's coming to him."

I smirked, not believing what he had just told me and that he was here at this time of the night. It was nice having him take me back home every evening, and even better being able to talk to him like two normal citizens of New York, but of all the things I expected to happen between him and me, this wasn't one of them.

An idea flashed into my mind. "I have something for the pain. Wait here."

I stood up in a shot and was going to hurry to the cabinet in the bathroom when he said, "No need. Thanks for worrying, but I think you are going to need the pain medicine more than me." He stood up and continued, his hand not clutching his belly anymore. "It was nothing. I'm going to get that son-of-a-bitch and teach him a hard lesson."

I weighed the option of stopping him, considering I knew his pain hadn't faded yet, but he just sprinted and rounded the corner before I could as much as step forward to halt him. His racing footsteps faded in the darkness of Brooklyn seconds after, and all I could do was to sigh.

Angelo was so disinclined to let me help him. He had been helping me for so long already I wished I could retribute the favor one day.

Angelo

I ran on the cracked sidewalk after him. John promised me the guns. Why the hell was he running away from me? I zipped past by one light pole to the next, the wind kissing my cheeks and lifting the lower end of my leather coat.

Halting, I glanced at one side of the corner of the block, and then, at the other. I found nothing. There were no signs of him. It was as if he had turned into a ghost or something like that. A short, soft sound echoed, and I snapped my head in its direction. A wall stood a couple of feet from me. Behind it was a house. The windows of it had long been broken, and dust had settled in.

If it weren't for the outlandish little noise, I wouldn't have bothered to give it as much as a look.

But I knew that shadow. It lasted nothing more than a second before dashing out of existence. I rushed to the door, tried it while throwing my weight against it, barged with my shoulder, but it didn't budge.

Fuck.

That motherfucker wasn't going to foil me now, and where was he going anyway?

I shot a look to the side and dashed to the half-broken window. Cutting myself or not by doing this, I was still going to do everything to get to him.

He guaranteed me the guns, after all, and I was going to have them one way or another.

I jumped through the window, rupturing it into pieces, and barrel-rolled before shooting my head up to take a long look around.

This was the living room, as I suspected it was. A solitary couch, worn by time, stood in the middle of it. The TV was an old Sony CRT model. No light bulb stood hanging from the ceiling, and there was a thick layer of dust all over the interior.

It was like having just trodden into the lair of an infestation of cockroaches, and the stench was just as bad.

I stood up as I tallied the seconds and trained my ears for any stray noise that might happen to occur. The house wasn't big – it had nothing more than a couple of rooms, but I still needed to keep my guard up.

I chased John from Manhattan to here, and if I knew him well, he had a plan, and it wasn't going to be good for me. I lifted my arms over my head and challenged, weighing each of my words, "John, I only need the guns, and then, once this is over, you and I won't have to talk again."

Silence. He didn't want to talk. I continued ahead, making sure to catch any noise – anything that might give away his location. I was content I wasn't panting anymore. I chased him through some blocks in my car before he finally crashed against a tree.

The woman in the house behind it had then shouted something in Russian, and neither of us had paid any attention to her.

To be honest, I couldn't care less that we ended up ruining her endearing Japanese garden.

I put another foot frontward.

The wood creaked. Through one of the doorways, John popped out, going as fast as he could, his Desert Eagle pointing at me, and pulled the trigger. The outcome of this flashed through my mind, and I thought that this was it. I was going to die, and I wasn't going to marry Alide after all.

CHAPTER 9

Discovering Each Other

Alide

I jumped, throwing my whole weight with me, and brought Angelo down with me. I came here just in time. I had just a glimpse of the white man in a white sleeveless tee pulling the trigger, and it was all the proof I needed to intervene and save him. This time, I was saving him from certain death, and doing so meant so much to me. He and I both collapsed on the filthy, battered floor with a loud thud, puffing out some of the layer of dust. He got up in an instant and looked at me like he couldn't believe what was happening.

He had very little time to react, though.

The guy he was chasing and fighting was already zapping his gun at him. "Get down," he shouted and shoved me with him to fall behind the couch. The shot exploded in the air and ricocheted against one of the walls.

His hands found my face like he couldn't believe my presence here and, to be frank, neither did I.

But I needed to do this.

He made me curious.

I felt pulled to him like he was a magnet. At this moment, I felt like kissing him. Time had stilled, and it was just us now. But I had very little time to think about that, ponder the costs and imagine what being more than his waitress would be like; the bald man with a blond beard was already firing at us again.

We scurried to the other end of the couch, my hand feeling so filthy thanks to all the dirt on the floor. More gunshots exploded in the air, and I grew aware of the bullets puncturing through the material of the couch.

I needed to do something, but what?

I had no idea. All I knew I needed to do was to stay close to him for as long as possible.

At this moment, anything could happen and, most all, I didn't want to lose my life or him.

We had a chance to become more than colleagues, after all. He scurried to the other side of the couch, and I could feel his mind was considering something. He shook his head and murmured, "Stay here. I'm going to kill him."

Fuck. It was like a vice was gripping my heart right now. He was risking so much when he didn't have to.

But that's what made him so knight-y right now. It was like I was living a dream of mine, where I finally had a man willing to sacrifice his life for me.

Time stilled for me again, and I covered my heart with my hands.

I just admitted he was my knight. *My King*, and I was his Queen.

He jumped, rushed to the other wall, and more bullets whizzed past him. They got so close. I imagined they were going to kill him. That's a thought I couldn't control, couldn't consider again.

It wouldn't happen.

For one very simple reason, it wouldn't. Angelo was one of the best shooters in the city, and he was going to bring that man to his due justice. Of that, I was sure.

But there was a barrage of bullets trying to kill him. The man with a blond beard and bald hair kept shooting his pistol, and it felt like it had infinite ammo. Didn't he have to reload or something like that eventually? I was so imprudent and ignorant when it came to guns. I knew nothing about them.

Angelo tried and tried to pop out to aim and shoot in a flash at his target, but the guy was relentless. I felt so useless right now. I was sitting on my own legs, behind the couch, and the other man, who kept shouting all kinds of obscenities, just couldn't stop shooting.

I needed to do something.

I spun my head around, trying to figure out something – anything that could bring him down. Anything to take his attention away from Angelo, who I shouldn't be thinking of as a possible lover of mine, but still did.

I needed to be useful one way or another.

I needed to help him when he needed me.

That's when I found it. A small boot. It was brown and worn. Whoever used it didn't care about it anymore. If I could...

I snatched it and popped my head over the couch. Angelo shouted something, but it was too late. The guy with the blond beard zapped his arm to me. He was going to pull the trigger.

Maybe I was going to make it.

Maybe not.

Too late.

I hurled the boot to him. Just when he squeezed the trigger, it hit his forehead. His head was forced to jerk backward, and he stumbled. I popped my head back behind the couch and prayed I did the right thing.

An explosion shook the atmosphere.

I whizzed my head in the direction it came from.

Angelo was now positioned past the wall he was hiding behind. His hand was holding his pistol, and a line of smoke was meandering out of it. The man he had been chasing fell down on the floor with a soft thud. On his face was an expression of bewilderment mixed with thanks.

Thanks?

I had no idea why the thought traversed my mind, but there was no denying I had that impression. That half a smirk was not the kind of thing someone did if they didn't want to die, after all. I slowly ascended and didn't know what to do with my hands and legs.

Angelo hurried up to me and asked, "Are you okay? Did he hurt you?"

I smiled, not knowing how to react. "No, he didn't. Thank you for saving me." He looked dazed, like he didn't expect at all my showing up here. And to be honest, neither did I.

Before I knew it, I was already running on the streets to get here. I sensed that something horrible was going to happen.

It was like a premonition.

He didn't smile back, and I hoped he had.

"That's good. I... thought for a moment he was going to kill you."

He had grabbed my hands and now finally withdrew them. It was like he forgot he had done that. I could almost chuckle now, but didn't. I felt that doing that, in here, wouldn't be a good thing.

"Are you okay, though?" I asked. "It felt like you really wanted to kill him."

He threw his hand in front of him dismissively. "No, nothing like that. I was just– I only need the key he must have with him. Still don't really know why he was running away from me to begin with, though..."

My heart was racing. The whole thing was crowded with adrenaline.

Still, I leaned down on the wall, crossed my arms over my chest and expressed, "Maybe he was just afraid. You are a scary guy after all."

He snapped his head to me, and on it was a smile.

And it was cute. It was shiny.

I smiled again too, not believing a moment like this one was bringing us closer together. It was like being in one of those romance movies I didn't like much.

But now that I was thinking about them... Maybe they weren't so wrong after all about where romance could lead a girl like me to. He walked to the man, squatted beside him and said, "You shouldn't have done that. I thought we had a deal..."

He was conversing with himself. It felt like his mind was scarcely cognizant of me now. When I minced to him, that changed. The sound of my footsteps was very faint, but he still heard them just fine. Maybe that was just his battle-hardened mind speaking, but I took it as something else.

I took it as a sign he wasn't the stubborn, uptight man I'd rumored he was.

I considered it as an indicator of a possible bond between us. Still, I decided not to act on it at the present moment.

Why would I anyway? This was being so good to us. The dead man now didn't even matter much to me. It was like I couldn't care about him anymore.

His head turned slowly to me. "Look, you are not supposed to be here. I don't want you getting involved in this kind of thing."

"And what is this kind of thing?" I dared to ask.

He exhaled. "It's not for you."

I supposed he was going to tell me something else, but he didn't. His hands went under the shirt of the man. He was looking for a hidden pocket of sorts. But he found nothing. He scavenged then the pockets of his pants.

It almost seemed like he wasn't going to find anything, until his eyes flashed.

Ah. He'd found something, and it was a key.

"What is it for?" I questioned, cocking my head.

"As I said, this is none of your business."

The line struck me as cold, and I quickly stood up and dusted off my pants. No point putting my job at the Bello Italiano at risk.

Luca needed me so much, after all. He led me to the door. I turned and put my hand on his chest. It felt wide. It felt like it was made of steel.

And most of all, it felt like it was made for me. Maybe the act was being seen by him as something I shouldn't be doing, but I thought little of it. I could probe a bit further, right?

Just a little more. It shouldn't hurt him.

"You are not going to leave that guy dead in here, right? You know nobody is going to come for him," I advised. I didn't feel like having some neighbors complaining about a putrid smell in the coming hours.

He shook his head and walked past me.

It was like he didn't care about that man at all.

The act alone should have taught me one more thing about Angelo's character, but if there was, it zipped right over my head like a bullet.

"I don't care about him. He got what a traitor like him deserved."

"Wait, he's a traitor? What did he do?"

He spun to me and barked, "Like I said, *it's none of your business.*"

I halted. I was going to say something else, but this time, I decided not to be nosy. It felt like going against my instincts, though, and it was a hard thing to do.

Being nosey throughout my life, after all, bore me many fruits, but I knew that doing it was pushing too further. His stare on me was cold. He couldn't believe I was trying to involve myself with the dark side of his life.

It was with that thought in mind I lowered my head and walked to the sidewalk in front of the house. In the distance, I perceived Manhattan and the taller buildings of Brooklyn. The Empire State building was like a beacon among all the others. And the One World Trade Center was even more than that.

In stark contrast, there were no buildings nearby. The locale was devoid of life. Not even grass wanted to grow here.

He started down the sidewalk, and I asked, "You don't have your car with you?"

"No, I'm going to have to call Prudenzio to pick me up, wherever he is."

Wherever he is? Had something occurred?

"Is he okay?" I questioned, trying not to sound too worried.

"He should be."

A moment of silence. I thought about asking him to stay with me in my home for a couple of hours, but decided not to.

That would be too weird.

He halted. There was a moment of unnerving silence. Was he going to kill me now because I knew too much?

Doing so would be so easy for him, after all. I was nothing more than a sitting duck on this cracked sidewalk.

"Thanks for helping me out here." He smiled. "See you tomorrow at work."

I gulped. I thought he was going to kill me, but he didn't. His hand didn't even edge near his pistol. It was tucked in his waistband, but there it remained.

He continued down the pavement. His soft footsteps were the only things that shattered the peace, other than the sound of the distant traffic. The wind kissed my legs and my arms, but I was scarcely paying attention to it. The ocean waves crashed against the shore, but again, I didn't care about it.

Because, there was only one thing that mattered to me now, and I also didn't know how to act.

It was like being in a distant plane of existence.

Ultimately, his silhouette disappeared in the fog that enclosed the neighborhood. I pictured myself running at him to ask more questions, but decided not to once more.

He had shared enough, and I was satisfactorily smart to know I could then be meandering into a dangerous territory.

It was the kind of place someone like me should never get near to.

CHAPTER 10

An Offer of Loss

Angelo

Of all the things I'd expected to happen today, this wasn't alone. Another lead squandered, and now, here I was. In her house. The other time, which was like weeks ago, I didn't get inside it. I had nothing more than a glimpse of it.

I stumbled upon her house. I was chasing him.

I was chasing Vinicio. I saw him. I was all alone. I couldn't call my friends, or else he wouldn't have managed to escape me. One moment he was right within my grasp, and the next.

Well... the next he was like a mile away from me. Damn, was he fast when he needed to.

I had no idea how he managed to get out, though I did see some Ancelottis with him. They were chasing him. If they were going to catch him again, I had no idea, but they better not.

Or else, I was going to come for them. Alide found me for the second time by her house. At least, this time, I wasn't right in front of her porch. This time, she found me on the next block. It was kind of some interesting luck to have her find me when I needed someone to aid me.

She offered me her hand, and I couldn't even walk. I had to put my arm around her shoulders while she brought me to her place.

"I'm going to thank you for this somehow, Alide, but I don't want to feel like a burden right now."

As we clumped ahead, she smiled.

It was the most angelic smile I had seen in my life.

Very bright, like the reflection of the sun on the ocean.

And her hair... Despite the gloominess of Brooklyn at night, it shone so gently. Everything about her just felt right. She took me to her home. A woman, who I took to be Rita, and then quickly confirmed it, ushered us inside. On her face was an expression of shock. She didn't think her friend, who was like a daughter to her, was going to bring someone like me in.

I knew I was dangerous.

People like her knew what I was like the moment their eyes landed on me.

"It's fine, Angelo. You don't need to thank me for anything. Working for you is already good enough."

She put me on the couch. My whole body hurt so much. I shouldn't have rolled down that plaque – or whatever it was called – when I didn't even know what was going to happen to me.

Vinicio was just so much nimbler, and maybe he even knew the layout of the place beforehand. That would explain a lot.

I shifted on the sofa and Alide went to a room to do something. I questioned myself what it was, but didn't have time to come up with an answer. She then came marching with a box of medicine packs. She opened one, and Rita, whose eyes were still as wide as before, brought a glass full of water.

"Thank you, you two. I don't know how I can repay this."

Alide giggled softly, and it came out like the most adorable thing I'd heard the whole day. Just one of the many reasons why I shouldn't think about involving her in my life more than she already was, I thought.

Although, with dad still so intent on making her marry me, maybe I wasn't going to have much of a choice.

"Don't worry about that right now. Just drink this, and you will be good in no time."

In no time? I didn't know about that. I was wishing I could stay here for a lot longer.

Too much longer, in fact. I put the pills on my tongue and gulped it down with some of the water in the glass. I gave it back to her, and just when I thought about resting on the couch for a little bit, my eyes caught sight of something that petrified me.

It made me feel so bad for her.

It was the little boy - the same one she was taking with her to GameStop.

He was rubbing his eyes with his fingers, and it was evident why he was doing that. He was in his soft blue PJ's as he padded to the kitchen, and in his hand he had a phone. At other times, someone like him would be taking a Teddy bear with him.

Like I used to, back when I was his age, I recalled.

He went to the sink, filled half of a glass with water from the faucet, and gulped it down. When he turned, his eyes finally landed on me.

And I just remembered why seeing him petrified me a little.

He looked so skinny. His cheeks were sunken in, like he hadn't eaten for days. I took a good look around the place. No wonder she was desperate for the job, I concluded.

They barely had a light bulb in the living room. The kitchen's stove looked like it had been through hell. The trash bin was almost empty, as if they never wasted anything. The floor was made of cement. It should have been finished a long time ago. Overall, this wasn't a place for someone like her.

And despite that, she was still a naïve woman who didn't worry about much.

I envied that about her.

The little boy's eyes fell on me. He halted for a second, and then waved his hand with a shy smile on his face. *Excuse me, because I need to sleep.* I could almost hear him saying that. But all he did was to close the door to his room.

At least the door they still had.

"So rude," Rita was speaking, "He should have introduced himself. I'm going to get him and fix that right now."

She began to trot to the little boy's room, but I raised my hand and said, "No need." I smiled too, for good measure. "He's probably just feeling tired."

She looked like she couldn't believe what I'd just said, but she still calmed down and seemed to understand that there was no point.

Alide approached me and denoted, "He's just Luca. He has school tomorrow morning. He's a good kid."

"I can see that."

I then weighed this one thing I thought about asking her.

Should I get involved in her life?

Was it fair? I'd been pushing her from mine because I didn't want to hurt her.

But yes. It was fair, if she needed me.

"Is there something wrong about him? If you need anything, I can help. I'm your employer, after all, and I want to make sure you're alright."

Rita seemed like she didn't know what to do with her interlaced fingers. I knew what was going on in her mind. She wanted to ask so many questions, but decided not to. For now, anyway.

Alide opened that same cute smile and sat down beside me. "He's okay. Sometimes, he worries me, but as long as I have the waitress job, he will be fine."

I jerked my head to her, seeming agitated. "If there's something going on, something you need my help with, you can tell me."

And I regretted my choice of words immediately after.

Yes, I should have made that question, but not in that manner.

I sounded too desperate, and even Rita grasped that, because she immediately darted to the outside of the house, where she lit up a cigarette and began to smoke. She shook her head. "It's nothing, really."

I could see she was struggling with something, though, and I didn't feel like dropping the subject. Out of instinct, I grabbed her hand. It felt warm – very warm – and so soft. It was like something intended for the Gods only.

I knew I shouldn't be doing this, but I didn't jerk my hand back. Doing this felt *right.*

And hey, it wasn't like I was telling her about the marriage or something like that.

"I can see he's struggling with something. He looks ill and weak. I can pay for his treatment," I insisted. Her eyes shot wide and then she withdrew her hand in an instant. Fuck. I made another mistake. *Another woman who's going to despise me for the rest of her life is born.*

She shook her head and looked away. "It's nothing, really. You don't need to worry about him."

"I know you care about him, but I also know how poor you are. You can't pay for his treatment, and you helped me. That man could have killed me, but you were there to risk yourself for me. That's something I can't forget."

She looked at me like she couldn't believe the words that just came out of my mouth.

And to be honest, neither did I.

However, I knew that this was the right thing to do.

She exhaled. "I don't really know what's going on with him. He coughs. Most of the time, there's no blood involved, but other times, he coughs it out too."

When Alide turned her head to me, she was shedding tears. "And I don't know what else I can do to help him now."

It was as if she was defying science, but in her crying, she looked even more stunning.

Even more picturesque.

And I caught myself looking at her like an idiot.

I was falling in love with her and I couldn't influence anything of that. It was like falling into a black hole. I patted her shoulder. "Say no more. Tomorrow evening, come with me. I'm taking you two to the hospital, and he's going to get the best treatment possible."

She stood up from the couch in a flash. "No. Thank you, but it's too much. I can't accept it."

In light of what was occurring, I was glad Rita was outside.

I stood up and grunted. My body was hurting so much.

I pulled her to me and hugged her. I let my head rest on top of hers. "It's nothing. You wouldn't be taking advantage of me. I'm the one making this decision."

She looked at me with wide eyes, like she couldn't believe what she had just heard. Likewise, I also couldn't believe any of this. And yet, I was more than certain I was doing the right thing.

I was telling her it's fine. I could do this, and then... We would see what would happen.

I felt bad for Luca, and this was a good chance to make the marriage more palatable.

Maybe I could think of it as a way to show her I wasn't such a bad man after all.

In a moment, her eyes locked with mine and her hands grabbed mine.

"I'm going to forever be grateful to you."

And I knew she was going to be.

* * *

People perambulated in the waiting room. Some were sitting on their white benches, their faces either expressions of depression or confusion.

Why is she ill?

Why is he here and not at home with me?

I could almost hear them asking that.

I was also waiting here, with them. Alide was with me, sitting beside me. I couldn't stop thinking about her smell. We talked so much. She told me what her life was like.

It was brutal.

She grew up without a dad.

And I began to realize why my father was so intent on making me marry her.

More than anything, she needed someone to keep her family safe.

Her Rita friend wouldn't be with us for much longer. Not only was she a heavy smoker, but she also couldn't stop eating fast food and other fat-heavy meals.

Alide's hand was holding mine on top of her thigh. Just like that, we had grown closer together in a matter of days. The ball of snow rolled down the hill, and now it was uncontrollable.

I knew where this was leading to, and I didn't know what to think of it anymore. Just one thing was important to me now, and that was making sure Luca was going to come out of this well. I had no idea what he had, but this was the best fucking hospital in New York City.

If it had a cure, I was going to pay for it.

And I knew how expensive hospitals here were. However, the fee didn't matter.

That was fine, though. For her, right now, I felt like paying anything and everything. To see the gleam of happiness in her eyes again, I was willing to spend all the savings I had. And I had regarded her as nothing to me once. That felt like a long time ago.

As she held my hand, I couldn't help but feel how soft hers was. Her fingers brushed mine every so often. She was looking without purpose on the floor, and her face was a painting of pain. I caressed her hand back. I couldn't let her think she was alone.

She wasn't.

I was here, for her.

"You think he's going to be alright?" She finally asked. This whole time she didn't say anything.

I squeezed her hand slightly. "Yeah, he'll be. He's a brave boy and he has the best sister in the world."

She chuckled. "I could have been better. I wasn't there enough for him."

"Hey, it's okay. You did your best."

She sighed and sat up straight on the bench. "My best wasn't enough."

A moment of silence while I weighed what to tell her. I needed to let her know she wasn't alone here.

"This is the best treatment he can have. If there's a cure, he will be okay."

"I hope so," she said before turning her head and locking her eyes with mine.

We were growing closer together, and I could only hope what this meant for me. Were we going to marry? Would she be happy with me?

So many questions, and so few answers as well...

I felt like giving her a kiss of comfort right now, but that's when the doctor stepped into the room and ushered us to follow him. Some of the parents and friends in the waiting room lowered their heads in disappointment. They thought he had come here for them. We followed him, and he led us to his office.

It was as sterile as everything else in the hospital. There was no speck of dust in it, and it was so brightly white it made me feel like I was going blind or something like that.

He sat behind his desk and gestured for us to sit down, which we did.

Alide had no idea what to do with her hands, so she kept interlacing her fingers.

The doctor cleared his throat. "Luca Mazzanti will be alright." Her head snapped to me, eyes gleaming with pure joy. "That's the first thing you should know."

His voice was somewhat unsympathetic, but I could feel he was enjoying this.

He had more good news for us, it seemed.

Alide could have squealed out of pure joy if she wasn't in this hospital.

"He's okay right now and will continue to have a happy life. There is one thing you need to know, though, and it might cost you a lot."

"Anything, doctor. I can pay for everything," I piped up. He glanced at me, nodded, and returned his attention to Luca's sister.

"He has a condition," he orated, and then explained what it was called, but it went over my head. To be honest, I didn't care about the name of it. "He will need to continue taking his pills for the rest of his life. There is no way to cure it. That's... the bad news I have for you."

His eyes were locked with Alide's, and I knew she couldn't take her eyes off him.

She needed to listen to every detail.

Everything mattered to her right now.

Alide glimpsed at me and returned her attention to him. "As long as he's happy and healthy, I'll be happy too."

The doctor nodded and cleared his throat again. "He will need to take some extra medicine too. It shouldn't be too expensive, and it will help him a lot."

A moment of silence before he continued, "He will just have to live with it for the rest of his life, and for the most part, he won't even be bothered by it. Once he has the medicine I'll be prescribing shortly, he will feel much better and happier."

That's good, I thought.

The little boy looked so depressed the few hours I got to know him.

The doctor then covered some things, and Alide and I proceeded out of his office. Luca was going to stay here for a while longer, under observation.

He did assure us many times he would be okay, and so, we had nothing to worry about.

We walked to the patio. A restaurant, tables and chairs made of wood decorated it. Some people were already here, and more were coming. We cogitated having a bite to eat.

And just as I said before, I was going to pay for it as well.

Alide looked so uncomfortable in front of me, and I wished I could hug and kiss her right now.

"Thank you so much for all this, Angelo. I don't know how I can repay you, if I'll ever be able to."

I looked for her hand and caressed it. "No need for that. Saving a boy's life is the least I could have done."

"It still isn't right. I should be able to provide for him by myself."

In a flash, I settled my hand on her chin before I could even comprehend what doing that meant.

Too late for that now.

Her eyes locked with mine again.

The patio stilled.

I couldn't care about the people here anymore.

Her eyes trembled, and I thought about kissing her. I needed to do it, but I felt it would be too sudden, and I hadn't even told her anything about the wedding. Did it even matter right now? Very much so.

"I'm here, for you and him. Don't hesitate to come to me anytime you need anything."

And that's when I knew I was making the right choice. I was going to marry Alide Mazzanti.

CHAPTER 11

A Desperate Chance

Alide

Ever since he helped me with Luca, I'd been asking if we had a chance. He was so intent on making sure I was going to have everything I needed now. He even asked his father to bump up my salary, which he did. I now made more than enough to have a comfortable life. I still lived in Brooklyn though. I had friends there that meant a lot to me, after all. And there was also the fact I just didn't have the money for a new place, though I was saving for it already.

And Luca now had plenty of games.

His cheeks were redder now and he put on some weight since coming out of the hospital. The medicine was doing wonders for him. His coughing was less frequent now. I could almost forget he had that illness.

I was wiping the table clean, removing the pieces of food still on it when something or someone slammed the door open. I startled and yelped.

In stumbled none other than Angelo, whose shirt and coat were all bloody. I yelped again, and dashed to him.

I ran as fast as I could do.

I needed to save him. His eyes were barely open.

He stumbled once more, and fell down on the floor. His face was directed to me, and I knelt before him and felt so useless. I yelled for someone to come, but the seconds passed and nobody did.

I was all alone with Angelo.

And he was bleeding so much.

Blood still tainted and spread in his clothes. He was barely breathing. He needed to be bandaged up and then have the ambulance blast its way to here.

He needed to be saved.

I couldn't lose him.

I... loved him.

He tried to speak, and upon realizing how much he meant to me now, I stood up in a flash and rushed to my telephone. I had left it by the kitchen room so that it wouldn't distract me at work.

I dialed 911 and the voice of a woman spoke. "Please, get an ambulance at the Bello Italiano in Little Italy! My- there is someone here bleeding a lot and I'm afraid he won't make it!"

She said I should calm down and that an ambulance was going to come as soon as it could. I had no idea what had just happened to him, and it made me feel so powerless.

I rushed back to him and the only thing that mattered was doing something – anything – to stop his bleeding.

But I had no bandages.

I had no nothing to stop his hemorrhage.

And despite that, I still thought of something. I didn't know if it would work, though, and didn't care. Doing that was better than just waiting for the ambulance's late arrival.

I yanked one of the table's cloths after taking off the support for the candles, and hurried back to him. Carefully, I lifted his torso and encircled the linen around him.

I had no idea where the blood was coming from, and I felt so nervous I couldn't even stop to find it out.

I knew I should, but my mind was such a confusion I couldn't think clearly.

I just couldn't stop moving.

All I needed was to find a way to lessen his bleeding.

I tightened the tablecloth around his waist however I could, and my heart calmed down once I realized the bleeding had been somewhat contained. But he still needed help, and I couldn't wait for the ambulance to arrive.

That's when it finally did, the tires screeching in front of the Bello Italiano.

It was night outside, and people were opening the doors and windows of their homes to find out what was going on.

The ambulance's siren continued to wail, and the lights kept flashing and spiraling.

Someone asked me to move away. I did, stumbling my way to the other side of the room.

They hoisted him to a stretcher. One of the doctors – someone with grey overalls which had the hospital's logo embroidered on it, hurried over to me with a pen and a notepad in his hands.

He asked me a question. I couldn't answer it.

I kept opening my mouth, trying to tell him I didn't know what had happened.

But nothing came out of it.

I kept clutching my hands together while my legs felt like jelly. That's when Mr. Romani showed up. His eyes were firing with rage and worry.

"Not the hospital. You are taking him somewhere else."

He just came from a car and was pointing his fingers at them. His face was an expression of fury. He said some more things about where to take him, and the medical team looked lost, talking among themselves and eyeing Mr. Romani.

He approached me.

I felt like I had done something wrong, but I calmed myself down.

I did the right thing, even if that meant calling the ambulance when Mr. Romani had a better place for him. It was something to do with him not wanting to let the hospital ask his son questions they shouldn't.

He trotted to me, though I knew he wasn't entirely confident. There was something he wasn't liking about this at all.

"You are coming with me, Alide."

That was no question, but a statement. He wanted me to come with him, and I was glad he did. I needed to know if Angelo was going to pull through.

If he perished, I didn't know what I would do with my life.

And Luca needed him so much. He got inside his car with me, and drove us out of the city. A solitary, old building emerged in the distance. Inside it, a light bulb in a room cast light that penetrated the darkness beyond.

The ambulance followed us as it should. I imagined the people inside it were scared that something terrible was going to happen to them after this was over.

Mr. Romani parked the car and commanded, "I'm really thankful you called them. They said he wouldn't have had a chance had they not come in time." He stopped for a second, staring at the ambulance. "You are a good girl. I want you to know that."

I had no idea how to respond properly, only that I was glad I was able to help save Angelo's life. He nodded and the medical team took Angelo to a room in the building. When Mr. Romani opened the door, it was like finding myself in a different plane of existence. The walls were super white, a big light bulb cast light into the room and there were virtually no shadows. I could perceive every detail of the medical equipment and furniture. There was an examination bed by one of the walls, and everything the team needed for the operation.

My heart was still racing.

I had no idea if I should stay and help him.

I just hoped he was going to pull through somehow.

Mr. Romani grabbed my arm and took me out with him. He ran his hand over his face. "I have no idea if he will make it out of this alive, but they said he has a good chance, and I have you to thank for that."

"I just want him to live, Mr. Romani. He's been so good to me recently."

His eyes widened. "He has?"

Alarmed and assuming he was thinking I was taking advantage of Angelo, I stated, "He's been a good friend of mine. He's paying for my brother's treatment."

His eyes cleared up, and my heart rate slowed to normal.

Phew. I'd assumed he was going to fire me right now.

"Ahhh, that's good. It's really good," he declared.

A moment of silence. Should I ask him the question that's nagging me right now? Yes.

"Why, sir? If you don't mind answering..."

He fluttered his hand in front of him. "He will tell you. Just stay here for now. I've got some things to take care of."

He approached me and grabbed my hand. "I trust you with him. He needs someone who cares about him now, and you are the best person for that." I nodded and said thanks. He walked to his car and disappeared back to the city. We were so far from the city I wondered how we got here without Angelo dying.

We got lucky. Too lucky.

He couldn't endanger himself again, whatever was happening in his life.

I perambulated and searched the building until I found its ancient living room. The walls were cracked, the paint was coming off and had long lost its color, there was no light bulb in the support hanging from the ceiling, and a thick layer of dust covered everything.

I flipped the switch on the wall just to make sure there was no hidden light bulb in here, and upon finding out I was right, I walked to the couch, and sat down.

My hands covered my face.

What should I do?

I did the right thing, but waiting wasn't for me. It never was.

I was a woman of action, and I felt like I needed to help save him. The doctors said I needed to wait. Just like Mr. Romani emphasized, I should be here for him when he woke up.

And he would.

The minutes went by. I checked my phone every so often. Something needed to be done – I needed to be more useful than this – but all I could think of was to lie down on the couch and close my eyes.

It was the best way to kill time.

Just when I thought I was going to fall asleep, I felt something prodding my shoulder. I got off the couch in a flash, and someone gasped.

My eyes fell on the mask, the white cap on her head and gown. She was a nurse, and I immediately felt bad for the way I treated her. It wasn't my intention.

"I'm sorry. I didn't mean to frighten you," I said.

Beneath her mask, she smiled. "It's alright. I know you've been suffering because of him."

She took a step forward and continued, "I've got good news. He's awake and should be able to return to his normal life soon, though I do recommend him not getting shot again. The bullet almost hit one of his lungs."

My heart leaped. It was so close.

I needed to find out what he was doing. Maybe he would listen to me.

Or maybe not.

Either way, I needed to talk to him about what befell.

"Thank you, but I don't know your name."

"It's Lucia, but you don't need to remember it. I'm going now. Most of the medical team is leaving. Some will remain to make sure he will be alright, but yeah. This is goodbye."

She smiled and departed. I hurried to the old room retrofitted to become an intensive care unit, and crept the door open. I didn't want to scare him or any of the doctors and nurses still in his room.

A machine beeped constantly when I stepped into the room. One doctor and two nurses still were here, their hands holding notepads and writing stuff. The two nurses were talking to each other.

My eyes then found him.

Angelo looked weak – weaker than he ever was. His eyes were open and looked healthy, though. Noticing that brought a shred of hope to me.

I thought he was going to die, and I'd be lost without him.

My legs felt like they were gliding on the floor as I padded to him. The doctor mentioned something about not pushing him and bringing up sensitive subjects to the conversation we were going to have.

I nebulously said to him it would be alright and that all I needed was a solitary moment with Angelo.

He darted his head to the nurses and took them out with him. The door closed behind them.

I sat down by Angelo, and I couldn't believe how frail he looked. His torso was all bandaged up, and had thin tubes stuck inside his nostrils. Another tube punctured his wrist, and he could barely keep a smile on his face.

I couldn't take this anymore, and shed one tear.

I hadn't been this worried for someone since Rita's AVC.

"Hey, Alide. I'm alright. I'll be getting out of here, and I'll be right there with you in the Bello Italiano."

I shook my head. "I made a big mistake. I should have called your father instead. I had no idea you couldn't be taken to a normal hospital."

He scanned the room. "Yeah, it's my first time here." He paused, breathing. "You've got nothing to worry. You did the right thing."

"No, I didn't."

He moved his hand a little, but couldn't lift it.

"Look, Alide," he uttered and I gazed at his beautifully brown eyes. "It's been some time since you helped me in your home. This is becoming a habit. I promise not to show up hurt at your feet again."

I chuckled, not believing he was cracking jokes during a moment like this.

He was just so close to dying.

"I'm not counting. You can show up hurt in my house as many times as needed. I'll always do everything possible to help you." I drew in a large cloud of air. "I can't lose you, and it's not just because of Luca."

His eyes peered at me, like he couldn't believe what I'd just announced. And neither could I believe those words.

They just came out, faltering.

But spouting them felt like the right thing to do.

Losing him would be worse than dying.

"I'm glad someone like you exists in this world..." He said, but didn't elaborate on it. I pondered the option of asking him what he meant, but my mind was such a tempest of different thoughts.

I exhaled and stood up. "Well, I don't think you need me in here anymore. You need some rest and then-"

"No, Alide. Stay here with me. Just call the doctor and the nurses to come when you want, or else they will worry my father will kill them because they didn't do their job properly."

I chuckled and sat back down with him again. My hands were interlaced in between my legs.

With an audible stir, he meandered his hand to mine, and held it in his. "Alide, you mean a lot to me. I want you to know that."

Time stilled for me. What was going on here?

Was it really happening?

Was he declaring his love for me?

No, it couldn't be.

I was day-dreaming. Nothing more than that.

"I'm going to call the doctor and nurses," I stammered, trying to go to the door, but soon crashing against an impenetrable resistance.

And it was coming from him.

Angelo was still holding my hand in his. Gripping it this time, to be more exact. His eyes locked with mine, and at that moment, he spoke more through them than he ever could have done with words.

He loved me, and I should have realized that a long time ago.

There was no rejecting it. Angelo wanted me. And before I knew it, I was kissing him. I was kissing him like there wasn't going to be a tomorrow. He'd just declared his love for me, and it was the most charming thing in the world.

It was the kiss to seal our fate forever.

CHAPTER 12

Renewed Hopes

Angelo

That was the best night of my life, despite being on a medical bed and hurt to the point of not being capable of moving my limbs properly. It took me a long while to recover, but I did, and now I was as good as new.

No one was going to stop me now.

Prudenzio and dad came to visit me there many times. It was our private, hidden hospital room located in the middle of nowhere.

No one would be bothered to find out what was in the building, and nobody made it their residence. In the official records, it was said the place belonged to a magnate in the city. Not even the governor or the mayor would ever worry about its existence.

Prudenzio always mentioned how he needed me to come back so that we could continue our hurt.

And we would. Vinicio wasn't going to escape our grasp again.

Of that, I was sure.

Dad was his usual worried and nagging self. He kept mentioning how I needed to reveal to Alide the marriage and the truth about her father.

I was going to.

It just... It didn't feel right worrying her about that right now.

She had too much on her plate, and I didn't feel like ruining her life.

We were lovers now. I visited Alide in her house sometimes and we began to share many dinners. We talked about our lives, shared our secrets and became everything many couples out there wished to be.

Still... telling her about the wedding. It felt so impossible.

And so, I continued to postpone the truth.

We also dined and had lunch together. We kissed many more times, and each time, it felt different. There was something about her I couldn't find elsewhere.

As for Tiziana, I already told her we wouldn't be happening.

She was okay with that. She blurted she never believed in us anyway, which pained me, but only a little. We had never come close to kissing each other, and I hadn't met her often these last few months anyway, so that's probably why she never grew fond of me.

My bond with Alide was something much more durable and stronger than what I had with Tiziana.

It would last.

I stood in my room, thinking and wondering. When would Vinicio ever come back home? And when would dad stop trying to kill him?

And killing him was now the order, but I didn't believe it. It had been a long time. *Father will understand he's wrong. Vinicio is a good guy. He's family.*

He's just... misguided.

I had a photo of him in my hand. It was taken back when we were teenagers. We were playing soccer, and our team won. It was nothing more than an amateur match between neighbors, but still, it meant a lot.

It solidified our bond, and now... it was like it was hanging by a thread.

Outside, the moon cast its white light into the city. The occasional planes flew from the JFK airport, and their destinations were all over the world. A dog barked every so often in the distance, and almost no one perambulated the sidewalk in front of the Bello Italiano.

I shed another tear, and then another and another. Before I knew it, I was crying like a little kid whose father had beaten him up.

The door crept open, and in stepped none other than Alide! I attempted to hide the photo and my tears, but it was too late.

She was going to close the door, but I held my hand up, asking for her to stop it.

She did, and her eyes looked confused. She'd just evaluated that she shouldn't have seen me in my current condition.

Just a glance at the mirror over the dresser was enough to tell me I looked like a mess.

A complete mess with no chance to return to my normal self.

Not without Vinicio anyway.

"I'm sorry. I shouldn't have barged in," she said, and her voice sounded so adorable and sweet.

Her eyes locked with mine. She was studying me, thinking about what her next step should be.

Just come to me. I hoped that's what my gaze was telling her.

I pulled a drawer open and stuck the photo in there. I didn't need to continue feeling like shit right now.

Not when Alide had just come here and she was looking that stunning.

Her hair was tied to a bun, and she wore no makeup, but still... Few women in the world could match her looks.

Despite her black and white waitress' uniform, she was angelic.

Despite all the things that made her suffer, she had eyes that could make anyone feel alive.

"Come inside. I'm not going to bite you," I announced with a demanding tone.

She smiled and walked to me. I felt like holding her in my hands, but I didn't know how she would take that, and I didn't need to do it to show her my love.

We smooched and it felt like it was going to last forever. Her arms went behind my shoulders, brought me closer to her as our lips pressed more passionately together, and her tongue battled with mine for domination.

We were lovers, but there was still the wedding thing, and I was waiting until disclosing it to her felt natural.

I'd rather keep the arranged marriage thing a secret for now.

I broke the kiss and we still hugged. Her eyes unlocked from mine, and her hand reached for the drawer where I had hidden the photo. I made no attempt to stop her.

I shouldn't.

That's when I spoke. "Alide, there's something you need to know... about why I've been hurt so often recently."

She didn't say anything. Her eyes merely examined mine.

"I've got a brother. He's younger than me, and very misguided. He thinks... that we are all trash. He wants to get out of it, of this city and build a new life somewhere else." I paused to breathe. "To be honest, all I want is for him to be happy. Nothing more than that matters to me, but father... he won't give up on him. He just never will. He will hunt him down even if he goes to Syria or something like that."

Alide continued to gaze at me like she couldn't believe what I'd just said to her.

To be honest, I couldn't blame her. My whole life was a lot for her to take in, and bringing her into it was dangerous.

Still, I learned it was a danger worth fighting against. She meant so much to me now.

"It doesn't matter if you think I'm right or not, but for the time being, I'm going to continue battling to bring him back. That's my vow."

A moment of silence while she pondered my words. "Angelo... I had no idea. I thought it was... It doesn't matter anymore what I had thought."

"Yeah, it's all a mess."

I sat down on the bed with her. Her hand looked for mine and she held it.

I felt my eyes watering again. I'd never presumed I would, one day, have to tell her about my brother, and what hunting him down made me feel.

I felt devastated.

I felt overpowered.

And yet, I couldn't give up on him.

I thought I was going to break down before her when she, out of nowhere, held my chin in her hand. "You've told me so much about you, and I still feel like I don't really know you."

I chuckled and turned my head to the other side. "Just ask me anything you want. I'm an open book now."

She cupped my chin again and forced me to turn my head to her for the second time.

I felt like this was leading to something much better than me crying in front of her, and I was liking it.

I was cherishing the direction this was taking.

There was a fire in her eyes that was difficult to control.

And it was making me think about all the things I could do with her. Things that should be kept hidden in between four walls...

"You can tell me anything you want," she began to say, "I'm here for you, and there's nothing capable of separating us."

Out of nowhere, she dumped me on the bed and straddled me. I had no more than a second to think about what was going to happen before she leaned down to kiss me.

Her lips were passionate. Her tongue, even more so.

Her warmth throbbed from her body.

Her hands began to unbutton my shirt.

Her eyes closed after locking with mine, and I shut them as well.

I drank in her assault, and wished for her never to stop.

Oh Alide, you are so much for me now. You are my Queen.

You made me forget about being infertile, how I thought I wasn't enough for any woman, and that I didn't deserve your love. You showed me I was wrong all along about you. I should have known you were like this right after we met.

She kissed me again, her lips pressing against mine.

Her nose sniffed me. She was loving where this was going to.

Her hand glided down and found my shaft.

She was stroking it.

"You are daring me to do it," I murmured, sensing where this was going.

"I dare you to do it, and much more," she whispered to my ear.

Gone was the woman who looked so carefree all the time. Gone she was, but not for very long. Alide was still there. She was the woman I learned to love. I just never thought I would find myself in a moment like this.

Her hand delineated my pectorals, my abs, and she took off all my clothes. I took off her clothes as well. We needed all of each other, and nothing more.

Outside, the serenity made me think I deserved this.

I was all alone with her.

I pressed my lips against her lips one more time. The flavor was just so her.

I disheveled her hair. I felt its texture and the individual flocks.

Her forehead sweated and my whole body felt slick. This was going too far, and I was loving every second of it. I was drinking every millisecond of our lovemaking. She was on top of me still, and she was making me love her so much.

More than anything, she was going to become my wife, once I had the courage to tell her the truth.

Her beautifully light-brown eyes locked with mine again.

Her hand stroked my shaft to full mast.

Her breasts kept pressing and rubbing against me.

She looked so different now, as if she had been born anew.

I fumbled her ass and brought her even closer to me.

I then spun around and shifted positions with her. This was my turn to make her happy. She gasped and protected her mouth with her hands. I pushed them gently to the sides and kissed her yet again.

Her hand raked my back.

Her nipples hardened like boulders.

And then, I entered her. I became one with her then and there, and I didn't even consider using a condom. I felt it would only have gotten in the way anyway.

Her eyes were dark with her arousal and love for me.

She sealed them with mine.

I made love with her, and it was the best thing that ever happened in my life.

More than anything, I knew this was going to last.

CHAPTER 13

Sizzling Worries

Angelo

I squeezed the trigger. The bullet blasted through the dirty air and hit the man. He was one of the Ancelottis, and was hiding Vinicio from me. Ever since he escaped me that night after he shot me, he managed to hide somewhere else.

Where? That was what I was attempting to find out.

I lowered my hand and Prudenzio appeared from behind me. His hands were holding his pistol. It glistened under the light of the sun that penetrated through the windows of this abandoned compound.

"Boss, I didn't think you were all alone here."

"I told you to keep up with me. Now, let's search."

Search.

Yeah, right.

I doubted Vinicio was still here. No wonder father wanted him back so badly. He was good at hiding and not letting us get him.

We padded to the other side of the compound. A door stood there. It was semi-open, and I swung it all the way. The air puffed up the dust on the cement floor.

Prudenzio headed to the other side of the small chamber, where he then opened another door and walked through it.

It seemed he had found something.

I didn't care what it was. I had something more important to do here.

I needed a clue. Nothing more than that. Just one little thing to tell me where I could find my brother.

I was tired of playing cat and mouse with him all the time.

I took a step forward, and my eyes landed on a piece of newspaper. It was just left on the dirty and cracked floor. In the meantime, my mind was barely aware of the chirping of the birds outside.

They were acting like nothing of this mattered.

I wished I could be as carefree as them.

Their happiness almost reminded me of Alide.

She was the woman of my life, and I was thinking of telling her about the marriage. More than anything now, she needed to know about it. It wouldn't be right to keep it a secret for a day longer.

I picked up the piece of newspaper and read the title.

Infertile Man Who Became Famous On Twitter Parts With His Wife And Both Of Them Think They Will Never Be The Same Again.

My heart stopped for a bit. Infertile man. I had read his story before. This was a continuation of it.

He didn't break up with her because of his infertility, right?

I read on.

The wife mentioned how badly she wanted a baby. *It was the thing I needed the most. Without my baby, I feel wrong. But my husband can't give me one. He can't make me pregnant. I'm lost.*

And I need some time away from him.

I couldn't be sure now if they were the couple I had read about before. Did that even matter, though? The essence of the story was the same, regardless of the people involved in it.

Infertile man broke up with his wife.

She mentioned why.

And it was his infertility.

That's why I didn't put on a condom when I entered Alide. I knew nothing was going to happen.

She made no queries about my choice. Maybe she even knew why.

Perhaps, she was aware of my pain for a long time already.

Whatever was the case, the story brought a tear to my eye. I would never have a child of my own with Alide. She was always going to want one, and I wasn't going to be able to provide it to her.

I was an aberration. I didn't deserve her love.

"Boss, is everything alright?" Prudenzio asked, leaning in through the doorway.

I blinked to get rid of the tear. "Yeah, I'm fine. Come on. Let's get out. He isn't here."

"As you command," he remarked before heading out and proceeding to the Chrysler parked in front of the compound.

The place was surrounded by trees, grass and other kinds of vegetation. It wouldn't be long until nature finished reclaiming the place.

I sat behind the steering wheel. I had a lot to think about, and Alide did make me think I was right for her.

But was I really?

She still didn't know about my sterility, after all...

* * *

She took my hand and we left the statue. It stood proud and magnificent on top of the huge pedestal. It was a nice gift from the French, back when the Americans were fighting for their independence.

Back then, it was all that mattered.

Things were so much different and simpler during those times.

We walked down the stairs and headed to the circular area that surrounded the statue. It's where we had a path that provided us with an incredible view of New York in the distance. The One World Trade Center building stood proud on the horizon, and it made the Empire State building look small in comparison.

It was just so bad we couldn't visit it right now, though.

Alide would love to be able to see everything tiny from up there, I was sure.

We reached the aforementioned path that surrounded Fort Wood and continued on it. Alide was so happy she couldn't contain herself. She wasn't walking, but bouncing, like she had no idea how to behave herself in a place with so many tourists.

I was nearly asking her to stop it.

I didn't want the Canadians and Australians thinking less of us.

Of course, to them, we looked like normal American citizens.

We were anything but, but they still thought that. We didn't look much different, after all.

We stopped by the metal wailing leaned on it. Her hand was still holding mine.

"It's so lovely here."

"It is."

"You know this is my first time coming here?"

I turned my head to hers, and she giggled. "You don't need to look that surprised."

I shook my head. "Everybody who lives in New York eventually comes to the statue. It's like one of those things you simply have to do."

"Not me. I've been a Brooklyn girl my whole life, and the statue reeks of Manhattan and its arrogance. They always think they are so better than us Brooklyians.

Brooklyians? That was a new term to me. Maybe I was arrogant like everyone else in Manhattan.

Still, I wasn't going to admit something like that in front of her.

Not when we were sharing such a good moment.

The waves crashed shily against the structure and rocks of the island, and people of different backgrounds walked behind us. Most of them spoke different languages.

There was nothing quite like visiting the Statue of Liberty.

Well, to be honest, probably the statue of Jesus in Rio was more stunning, but this one wasn't a far cry from it.

"I'm not like them," I boasted.

She shook her head, either agreeing or disagreeing with me.

For a moment, I didn't know which to believe.

She then smiled, and I knew it was all okay.

Egotistical or not, she enjoyed my company.

Alide grabbed my hand and said, "Thank you for taking me here."

Seconds of silence ensued. We were admiring and cherishing the view in the distance. There was nothing quite like New York when it was being seen from here.

I was thinking about taking Alide to Chicago. That would give us a bird's eye view of this city and, also, of that one.

I was sure she would love it.

And then she expressed, "I was thinking... I would love to have a child."

She smiled. It was nothing more than an innocent dream thrown in the air.

She meant nothing by it.

But seeing the glee of content and hope in her eyes... I couldn't help but feel desperate.

How wrong was I? I wasn't good enough for her. She would think less of me and maybe... even dump me for someone better. *Someone who wasn't infertile.* I knew thinking that right now was crazy, but my mind was so paranoid.

And the worst thing about it?

It was that the suspicion wasn't unsubstantiated.

I had read and heard far too many stories of men who got dumped by their girlfriends and wives once they learned something about them – it didn't have to be the same problem as mine – that prevented them from forming a complete couple.

And the infertility thing... that was one of them.

I cleared my throat and she giggled. "If you aren't ready for it yet, it's okay. I was thinking about something else, in fact."

I kind of dreaded asking her what it was, but I did so anyway.

"I want to marry you," she said, and that's when I knew she was finally ready for the truth.

Alide

I told him about the marriage thing. I was just joking. Well, not joking that much, to be honest. There was a flake of truth to it.

I just didn't feel like telling him all of it.

Not when we were having a good time and I didn't want to worry him about other things. His brother, Vinicio, and dad were already enough on his plate. If anything, he needed my help.

And I was more than willing to be there to provide support for him.

The customers were now leaving the Bello Italiano. The sun was setting in the distance. We didn't keep it open until late at night. We did make pizzas and everything one could expect from an Italian restaurant, but this place was different.

It was more family-friendly, despite the Mafia owners.

Thinking that brought a smile to my face.

The place was growing serene. There was only an old couple sitting at one of the round tables. They were chatting like they had nothing to worry about.

And I knew what people talked about me.

"Oh, you always seem like you don't worry about anything."

But it was a misperception. I did worry.

A lot.

I opened the door to the back compartment of the Bello Italiano, where we had the kitchen and the offices. That's when I heard a grunt followed by a scream.

Was someone in pain?

I needed to find out what was going on.

If it was Angelo and he needed my help again...

The first thing I would do would be to call his dad. He made it clear I couldn't end up sending him to a normal hospital.

I hurried to where the screams and shouting were coming from. There were more people involved in the altercation.

Men were.

I halted in front of the door. It had a rectangular glass for a window in the top section of it. It was too high for me, but going on my toes was enough to allow me to peek at what was transpiring inside the room.

My heart vaulted.

Angelo and his old men were both standing in the middle of the room, and they were smiling.

Smiling like what was happening there was a good thing.

I raised myself higher on my toes and discovered something that made my heart stop for a second.

They tied a man to a chair.

He couldn't move.

One of his eyes was swollen and I questioned myself if he had lost it.

His face was brushed with bruises and cuts.

A line of blood was coursing from the corner of his mouth.

His head was lolled down.

They were torturing him.

I felt my legs weak, and then gasped.

Shit. I shouldn't have done that, and most of all, I shouldn't be here.

I rushed to the other side of the hallway and hid behind a wall. The door to the torture room crept open.

Someone must be, right now, sticking his head out to find out if someone was spying on them. The last thing I needed was Mr. Romani's wrath breathing down my neck. He could ruin me, and more than anything, I needed to stay on his good side.

I needed the money for Luca's treatment and medicine.

The door closed with a soft thud, and I exhaled. My heart was racing so much I thought it was going to burst through my chest.

I was sweating too. I didn't think I would ever witness something like that in my life.

Let alone in the Bello Italiano.

And here I was thinking the place was family-friendly. To people who had no idea what was going on in here, it was. *Ignorance really is a bliss, isn't it?*

I opened the door to the changing room and took off my work uniform. I changed back to my short jeans pants and red top before going out to wait for Angelo.

The sentence *wait for him* felt heavier in my mind now.

Despite being so lovely to me, there was no denying he was still part of a Mafia family.

The Romanis.

I almost forgot who I was dealing with this whole time. I shouldn't have let that happen. I should have always remembered he wasn't the kind of man I could mess around with.

I was sure he was more than ready to kill me and Luca if he needed to.

He was currently going for his brother's head, after all...

CHAPTER 14

Growing Uncertainties

Alide

I took a sip from my red wine glass and put it down on the edge of the roof of the building. The sun was setting in the distance, and dare I say, this was the best view I'd seen my whole life.

Even better than the one in Liberty Island, to be honest.

I could see the people walking on the sidewalks down below without a care in the world. Some were holding hands. Valentine's Day was approaching, so the citizens of New York – and of the rest of the country – were getting ready for it.

Cars ambled on the roads with a touch of serenity that impressed me. Little Italy's streets were narrow, and drivers needed to be mindful at all times.

Angelo took a drag off his cigarette and exhaled a large plume of smoke.

His arm was around my shoulders. He was warm and comforting, but there was something different about him.

And I should be honest with myself again.

Something was different about me too. I couldn't be all touchy and agitated with him like we usually were. Seeing him making a man suffer for information and pleasure punctured my mind with memories I thought I had long buried.

But it all came back.

It all sprouted to life again.

And now, I wasn't sure anymore I wanted to marry him.

Angelo hadn't done much already other than to have talked about the next movie he wanted to watch with me, Luca's progress, brushed over a possible marriage, and also mentioned some other more mundane things that escaped my mind at the moment.

I sighed a few seconds before he asked, "Is something bugging you?"

"No, I'm fine. Nothing is bugging me."

A moment of silence. He was assessing if he should push on.

Was he thinking the same thing?

Was he feeling I was distant too?

I didn't want to make him think that of me, but still... it wasn't like he was helping me.

"You know, if there's something you'd like to tell me, you should do so now."

"But I don't have anything to talk about with you right now."

He shook his head. "There is something you are keeping from me."

When he opened his mouth to say one more thing, I piped up, "I'm not hiding anything. I'm like an open book right now."

I smiled and hoped my smile was persuasive enough, but I had no idea if it was.

He turned his head to look to the horizon, where the heart of Manhattan stood.

A long moment of silence ensued.

"I just think we should be truthful to each other. Hiding something will only make things worse."

I studied my next words, and also his expression.

I couldn't turn this into him breaking up with me.

Most of all, I needed Angelo. I loved him.

"Well, there's something I have been avoiding to tell you..." I at last revealed.

"I knew there was."

I could rebuke him right now.

But decided to keep my mouth shut. For the time being, that was better.

"It's just that you are looking and feeling different today." I paused. "And to be honest, it's not just today. You've changed these last weeks."

He took another drag off his cigarette and blew the smoke out.

"I don't know what you are talking about," he said matter-of-factly.

"But there *is* something. Your eyes look concerned – more so than when there's something that involves your brother."

His pupils examined me for seconds, and I projected he wasn't going to reply.

That's when he proved me wrong.

"Did you ever ask yourself why you didn't become pregnant after that night?"

I shook my head. I didn't think about that. It was good – very good – but was there something special about it?

A tear rolled down his cheek, glistening under the moonlight.

"I am infertile, Alide. I can't give you a child."

I covered my mouth with my hand, almost gasping. A car's horn blared in the distance as someone shouted *figlio di puttana*.

I looked down, in shame.

So, that was why. Why he was different now...

I thought he was going to break up with me or something worse.

I didn't know he had to deal with something like that his whole life.

"I'm sorry. I shouldn't have pushed on."

"No, it's fine." He turned his head and there was a gentle smirk on his face. "I'm glad you've asked me about it."

I shook my head. "But it isn't right. You don't have to beat yourself up because of something like that." I settled my hand on his shoulder. "I don't need kids anyway to be happy with you." I opened a wayward smile. "Luca is already a lot on my plate anyway."

He chuckled. "C'mon. He's a good kid, and I know you love him."

I locked my eyes with his, gazing, and for a moment, seconds of mutual understanding ensued. He knew his condition didn't bother me, and I could almost forget about the torture thing he did a couple of days ago.

I wasn't going to forget it completely, though.

It was going to be in my mind for a long time.

But, for the time being, I could think of it as nothing more than a blimp in the life of the man I wanted to marry.

Angelo

I opened the door and sauntered down the hallway to my room. The sun was shining like a fiery jewel in the impossibly blue sky of the early Spring. My mind was almost not aware of the chatter of people outside the Bello Italiano as they ambled on the sidewalk. Adding to that, cars blared their horns in the distance to remind me where I lived.

And of course, there was a horde of pigeons cooing on the building's rooftop.

Damn them.

Alide had no idea how much I hated them, and if destiny didn't decide to fuck my life again, that wouldn't change.

At all.

I picked up her voice. It was so beautiful. She was talking on the phone.

I knew I shouldn't be doing this, but I was anyway. I leaned on the wall to overhear what she was conversing about.

Maybe this was my Romani side talking louder than the Angelo one, but I didn't feel bad about it at all. It just felt right to overhear her when she didn't know I was around.

"Rita, I-I'm not sure I should be telling you this."

Her voice sounded a bit startled, like she knew she was doing something wrong but still felt compelled to get it off her chest.

And I felt like gushing into the room to tell her she had nothing to worry about.

I was this close to telling her about the marriage. She was finally ready.

I hadn't done it before because I got caught up in some things I needed to do for my father. Hunting down Vinicio was hard.

In the meantime, I was glad my ears were good enough to pick up Rita's words.

"Girl, if there's something you need to tell me, do it now. I've got lunch to make for Luca."

Alide chuckled. Oh, the sweetest chuckle I'd heard in a long while.

To be honest, it was always like that. I was just so stupidly in love with my soon-to-be bride.

She exhaled. My heart stopped for a second.

"I was walking down one hallway in here a couple of months ago-"

"I can't believe you've been keeping that from me this whole time!"

Damn, Rita was a real piece of work. She didn't even let Alide finish her sentence before spouting that. And here I was thinking I had nosey friends.

"I know, but I had no choice. I wasn't sure I should tell anyone. But now..."

"You can't keep that in your chest anymore, right?"

A moment of quietness.

"Angelo and his father... They were torturing a guy in a room here. I'd never seen anything like that. Oh, there was so much blood and his left eye was swollen. I can still remember all the details as if it was happening in front of me."

Her voice faltered. So, it was her then. I thought it was just a rat or my imagination.

I didn't feel betrayed by that, though.

Her reaction to it, on the other hand, was like she had just punctured my heart with a needle.

Of course what she'd witnessed impacted her. *You need a strong mind to ignore how inhumane what I was doing to that guy was, after all.* I just necessitated the information he had on Vinicio – nothing more than that.

But of course, he had to be tenacious.

He was my brother's best friend. I never liked him much, so I didn't feel an ounce of remorse for what I did.

But overhearing Alide talking about it like it made me a monster was a different matter.

Was that what she was thinking of me right now?

Was I a degrading monster to her eyes now?

I couldn't believe it.

It just couldn't be happening.

Rita respired on the other side of the call. "I told you what those people are like. You think the restaurant is how they make money? It's just a front for their operations. They *kill*, *rob* and *extort* people. They've got roots in the Assembly and everywhere else. Those people aren't the bunch you want to involve yourself with. I *warned* you."

"You are not making this easier on me. I'm not breaking up with him. He showed me he's different."

"Is he? I thought you had said he was beating someone who couldn't defend himself. What kind of man do you think does that? What if you piss him off after you two are married? What if Luca angers him? What do you think he will do? You think he'll just let it slide?"

A moment of stillness. I wished I could get the phone and tell her she was wrong.

If Alide happened to anger me in the future, I wouldn't lay a finger on her. I wouldn't raise my hand. She was the love of my life.

I'd do anything to keep her safe.

"I'm not so sure. This was a mistake. I'm not talking about this again."

"Alide, you nee-"

But she ended the call before Rita could finish her line. They lived together, so I was sure she was going to have to listen to what her friend had to say one way or another.

Still, what she said.

It was right.

I slew and robbed people. Sometimes, they had nothing to do with anything.

Casualties – that's what they were to me and my father. He taught me not to care about people much. It worked for me all these years, but now, things were different.

I loved Alide, and she made me realize I needed her more than anything in my life – more than father, Vinicio and marrying someone who could make the Romani family stronger.

But Rita was mistaken.

Or was she?

Maybe I wasn't the right man for Alide after all...

*　*　*

The table clock ticked endlessly. Time was passing. The building had been enveloped by a veil of deafening silence. My fingers pressed the keys and my eyes scanned the pages on the screen of my laptop computer.

I shouldn't be doing this.

And yet, I was.

I couldn't stop thinking about it. I thought Alide had helped me beat this battle. She said she didn't care if we were going to have a baby or not, but after I overheard her talking to her friend about me being a monster...

It made me think.

And it brought me here.

My fingers were like ice stones as I pressed the keys. I was obsessed. I read one story about an infertile guy who broke up with his girlfriend who he first met back when they were just teenagers. I then skimmed a text wall of another guy who had written he couldn't even use Tinder anymore because he felt insecure about himself all the time.

And what's more, he also mentioned his cock was too average to make his dates happy.

Now that I was thinking about, Alide never commented on the size of my dick. Was it big enough for her? She seemed pleased the last time we did it, but I couldn't know for sure. Maybe she was hiding the truth from me this whole time.

Perhaps, she was just feeling pity for me.

And that's... too humiliating.

I read another story, and then another and another. The moon was behind the building back when I turned on the computer, and now it was standing almost in front of the window.

It was like it was watching me now.

And laughing.

Because I was a pathetic fool with low self-esteem.

It didn't matter how many compliments I got from different women. I could never gift a child to one of them, and that's something that would forever be in my mind unless there was some obscure treatment I didn't know about.

But there wasn't.

I was all alone with this.

I and these men were, to be honest.

CHAPTER 15

Was it Fair?

Angelo

I was sure she was wondering about this.

Am I ever going to adapt to his world?

What if he gets pissed off at me? Will he kill me then?

Every time we met since that afternoon I overheard her, I fought the urge to tell her I wasn't *that* man she defined on the phone. To other people, things were different. But she was like my retreat harbor. She was where I came to be someone different.

A better man.

If only I could tell her what was going on in my mind right now, though.

But I couldn't. It felt too painful.

I was sitting at one of the tables in the restaurant, my fingers interlaced in front of me. Father opened the door and stepped in. He halted, eyes examining me like I was a dead body in the morgue.

I was aware of his presence, but didn't dare to glance at him.

I knew what was going on in his mind now.

He knew about Alide and me. He was happy we were making progress and paving our way to becoming a proper couple. But I still didn't tell her about the marriage. I couldn't. It felt too painful. It felt almost impossible.

And after I overheard her calling me a monster to her caretaker, it was like a huge wall was built between us.

I just couldn't approach her and tell her we had this marriage thing to make happen, that her father meant it all along, and that he wanted me to provide for her, as a husband and the father of our child.

The father thing, though – he didn't know back then it couldn't be made to happen. He had no idea I was infertile. At the time, neither was I aware.

I was just a teenager in those years. Rock n' roll and fucking around were my things, not killing people and pondering impossible-to-occur marriages.

Father padded to me and put his hand on the table.

It felt like a rock had just fallen on it.

"Look at me, son."

"I haven't told her anything yet, father."

"Just look at me," he insisted.

I craned my head to lock my eyes with his. I thought I was going to find the rage of a man who was disappointed with his heir, but I unearthed something else.

Comfort.

Sympathy.

"I know what's been happening. I know you can't have children of your own."

My heart skipped a beat, and he waved his hand in front of him dismissively.

"I was aware of that since you were born. Her father knew it too. And despite that, he chose you for her. Do you know how much that means to me?"

A tear rolled down his cheek.

I didn't do anything. I couldn't even move a finger. It felt like ice surrounded my whole body.

"You don't have to prove anything to me. Just tell her the truth, and I'm sure she'll be with you. She's a smart girl and she loves you."

His hand seized mine. His fingers then foraged it.

"Do this for me and her. She needs you more than anything and anyone else in this world."

Slowly, my father receded his hand and walked away. After he opened the door to the sidewalk, his hand went up to wipe the tear on his cheek.

I'd never seen father crying in my life.

My infertility problem felt tiny in comparison to this scene.

And a crucial decision was then made.

Alide

I opened the door to Mr. Romani's office and stepped in. Uh, he's not here. I walked to the desk and immediately stopped.

I shouldn't be here if he's not around.

What if he finds me poking around things that don't belong to me?

And what was I even trying to find in this room? His letter telling me he was going to kill X citizen in the city or something like that?

This is not a place for me.

I turned and faced the door. I was going to walk out of here and forget I ever thought about snooping around, but that's when my eyes landed on a semi-open drawer not too far from his desk. It was full of paper sheets, and one stood out among them.

It did so because the title of the document was written in black, bold letters.

Our Agreement.

The first thing that made me curious about it was that the title and the font used for it weren't common for professional documents I'd seen in my life. It drew me to it, and that coupled with my tendency to poke around were motives good enough to make me pad to it.

I shouldn't be doing this was the last warning the rational part of my mind emitted before I pulled the drawer and picked up the paper sheet.

I read it.

And I began to cry one second later.

I couldn't believe my name was mentioned in it multiple times. Dad's name too. This was written just before he died, and it explained so much.

It told me everything, in fact.

Why did Mr. Romani and – Angelo – keep it hidden from me all this time?

Was this why I was hired in the first place?

My heart leaped. Tears rolled down my cheeks.

I couldn't wrap my head around this revelation and thus shoved the paper sheet back into the drawer like it was made of feces.

I then hurried to get out while my hands wiped the tears off my face. My shift was over, but the last thing I needed was Mr. Romani and Angelo finding me in here.

I just couldn-

The door opened, and in front of me stood none other than Angelo. His hand reached out to me, but I was past thinking he had come here to explain everything and make me think he wasn't to blame.

I tried to charge past him, but he didn't allow me.

His arms went around me and hugged me to him. I tried to punch him, but I was too feeble. I couldn't muster up the strength to just shove him off the way he deserved.

His mouth was opening and closing, and he was attempting to tell me something.

What it was, I couldn't care.

That's when I finally spoke, and my words were tainted with rage.

"I should have known! I should have known!"

"Alide, I've been trying to tell you, but it's been too hard for me. I should have been braver. I'm a weakling and I don't deserve your love."

His hands cupped my cheeks as he brought my eyes to meet his.

"I can explain it all. Just don't go right now."

"There's nothing to be elucidated. You hid it from me this whole time. You knew who my father was and that he wanted me to wed you!"

"Yes, that's what I was going to tell you. I just didn't have the courage. I didn't want to ruin you. You are so kind and caring. Being in my life is something completely different from what you are used to."

"To hell with your life! I need to go. I can't be in here anymore."

I threw my weight against him. Maybe that's what did it, maybe not.

Either way, it worked.

I managed to get past him and was running to the bus stop. I needed to get into it and flee from Little Italy to never come back here.

I was crying and feeling like when my mother died. It was as if hands were squeezing my heart forcefully. I couldn't comprehend how he had been capable of keeping the truth hidden from me for so long.

Did he think I didn't deserve it?

But of course he was able to do that.

He killed and tortured people. Hiding a wedding from his bride was easy peasy for someone like him.

I should have known there was something ominous with his family the moment his father hired me and how his father had then been so excessively kind to me, as if he'd known me all along.

Known me.

These people knew who I was, where I lived, my family and how poor we were. No wonder Mr. Romani had been paying me more than what we had agreed on. No wonder his son 'fell in love' with me.

It was all planned from the very beginning.

Our love was fake.

CHAPTER 16

The Wrong Choice

Angelo

I was a coward. Always had been. Vinicio ran away because I didn't dare to change father's mind. And I was hunting him down for the same reason. I'd always assumed I couldn't do something before anchoring said supposition in my mind.

And the worst thing about that?

It wouldn't change.

I was an idiot and a coward. I should never have approached Alide.

She was now hurt and crying. She bolted out. I comprehended that forcing to keep her here was the wrong thing that I could have done. Alide wanted to disappear from my life, and doing anything other than allowing her to fulfill that was wrong.

I was wrong.

I couldn't gift her a kid, and she wanted it so much.

I went to my bedroom while feeling like I was a zombie. I couldn't think about anything or anyone that wasn't Alide and our love. Her beautiful smile and face were in my mind all the time. I needed her, but she was right.

I was mistaken.

I should have been stronger.

I should have confronted my father.

I should have told her the moment she first came here who she was to me and that her father wanted us to wed. It wasn't my decision. It had never been. That's his choice, and mine was to obey him.

I did so because it was his last wish before he died, and it meant so much to me.

I didn't know how much time had passed since coming here. I'd collapsed on the bed and buried my face in the pillows.

The door opened, and I didn't care who had come.

Maybe it was Alide, ready to tell me she forgave me.

But that was just aspirant thinking. If anything, she could have come here to pick up something she forgot and wouldn't even glance at me. And I wouldn't blame her if she had such a reaction.

It would be the right and fair thing to do.

I should be nothing to her.

I thought so much I was doing the right thing...

"Son..."

Father. Of course it had to be him.

I could lash out at him and tell him he's the one who ruined Alide, but I couldn't. Doing it felt impossible, like killing your mother in cold blood. All I could do was to keep my head buried in the pillows as if they were going to swallow me whole at some moment.

"I saw her running away to the bus stop. She got into the bus before I could get out of my car." He paused, clearing his throat. "You finally told her, didn't you?"

I presupposed he was going to lash out at me, and he wouldn't be in the wrong. If anything, telling me I was a coward would be the fair thing to do at this moment.

I fucked things up.

I screwed it all up.

But he didn't persist. His hand shut the door, living me alone with my thoughts. And they were killing me from the inside out. It was like an immense flame was burning me alive.

And it felt like father had just given up on me.

I wasn't worth becoming the new Don of the family.

I am not his heir anymore.

Alide

I buried my head in the pillows and cried. Rita crept open the door and uttered some things, but I didn't pay attention to her. My mind had been consumed by what had happened. I should have known he wasn't right for me.

I should have buried into my mind that falling in love with someone that dangerous couldn't have become a good thing.

It never had a chance of being something different.

Reading that agreement between his father and mine was like unveiling a pile of shit someone painted to look nicer.

But, it wasn't and could never be.

My dad was wrong. We couldn't happen. One thing that pissed him off would be enough to make him kill me.

And Luca... he might as well be dead now.

The treatment was doing wonders on him, but without Angelo... I wouldn't have the money to continue paying it. The nice nurse who took care of him and became his friend would never see Luca again.

That was that.

And I wouldn't have money for his medicine.

Nor for his games.

And he wouldn't be able to buy another used game for his PS4.

I might as well be killing him now too. Angelo and me... we're the ones who crushed little Luca's hopes of having a normal life.

The door crept close. Rita tried and insisted some more, but I just didn't have the mind to talk to anyone right now.

I was sure Luca was asking now what was going on with me, and Rita wouldn't know what to tell him. Just that he should be strong because this was going to be temporary.

That was what I was hoping.

Because I needed to find another job soon.

And I needed to forget Angelo entirely. Thinking about him and remembering all the good times we had together was too painful.

I had no idea how much time had passed, only that the sun was now rising over the Atlantic Ocean. Its light penetrated through the dark red curtains and revealed the contours of the room.

I should be getting off the bed right now.

But I couldn't. There was so much happening, and staying here, lying on this bed was like being successful in running away from everything.

Maybe it was all going to fix itself soon.

Perhaps, I was going to learn it was nothing more than a bad dream in the end.

I hand settled down on my shoulder. For a moment, I hoped it was Angelo's. But it was much smaller and gentler. It couldn't be him, and yet, I was hoping so much he had come here to tell me he was wrong.

But he hadn't come, and he never would.

I'd do well to keep that in mind.

"Alide." It was Rita's voice, sounding distressed. "You need to eat. You've been sleeping for hours, and it's time for lunch. Luca is worried about you."

Luca.

I couldn't fail him.

I had to be there for him.

With a grunt, I sat up on the bed gradually. My body felt like it was made of granite, and my eyes hurt so much. Never before did I cry so much in my life.

"I don't want to talk about *him*," I announced right away because I didn't want to remember him. And I knew that expression on her face. She had a lot of things to tell me.

"First, let's have lunch," she declared with a small smile on her wrinkled expression.

With an uncomfortable smirk, I got off the bed and walked like a ghost to the door. Luca was standing right in front of it, his hands clutching his phone.

"Sis, I was super worried. I thought you didn't want to talk to me..."

I disheveled his hair, though doing that didn't feel like the other times I'd done it. It felt distant, like I was forcing myself to do it.

"Don't worry. I'm here and I'm okay. Now, let's have lunch."

A moment of silence. "I already had it..."

"Oh." I gave him a phony smile. "It's alright. I'll eat by myself then."

Rita took me to the kitchen table and said, "I haven't had lunch. I've been waiting for you to get up."

"I'm sorry. I shouldn't have been so selfish."

"You haven't been, but you'd do well to tell me what happened."

"It's... Angelo."

She nodded, an expression of clearness on her face.

"And you won't believe what I learned about him. My father vowed to make him marry me. They even have a contract with his signature and everything! I can't believe he kept it hidden this whole time!"

She rested a hand on top of the table.

"He wasn't the only one."

My heart skipped a beat. "You don't mean..."

"I do. Your father entrusted you to me until you were of age and could marry Angelo, but things changed. A lot happened, and you then turned 18, and Mr. Romani and I decided to stall the wedding until we felt you were ready." She gave me an uncomfortable smile. "I guess that having you work for him all these months must have changed his mind."

I took a step back, not believing what she was telling me

It wasn't enough that Angelo kept the wedding plans veiled from me all this time – she had been doing the same thing as well. Who else knew about all this madness?

Before I could think about doing something I would regret, she hurried to me and grabbed my hand. She then pulled a chair with force and we sat down.

Her hand was gentle as she held it.

The expression in her eyes exposed all she was thinking.

She did what she did for good reasons, and it wouldn't be right for me to bash her right now.

"I'm sorry I had to do it. Mr. Romani insisted that he wanted to make his son reveal the wedding plans himself. That's why I didn't tell you anything about them."

I didn't feel like withdrawing my hand, and I could understand why she did what she did.

All these years she cared for me and Luca when I didn't have another family. She didn't do it to hurt me. She did it to protect me.

In a flash, she removed her hand and rested both of her forearms on the table, eyes looking out to the side yard. "But if you want to hate me, I'd understand. I made a mistake and I should pay for it."

And in that instant, I cried.

I broke down.

I wept.

Luca was standing by the doorway. I was aware I shouldn't be looking like this to him, but I just... couldn't stop. Sadness and remorse were obliterating my mind.

Rita put her arm around my shoulders and kept me close to her until I'd stopped crying.

I wiped my tears with my hands and stated, "I understand why you did it."

Her eyes widened. "You do? I thought you were never going to forgive me."

"No, I do. I'm sorry if I made you feel that way."

A moment of pause as she digested my choice.

"Alide, let's have that lunch now, okay?"

I smiled back. At least when having lunch I could forget about Angelo and his betrayal.

Food was always a good medicine.

I dug in and finished my plate in less than five minutes. Never before did I eat so fast. Maybe that was just the rage within me speaking. Whatever's the case, her lunch made me feel better. By the time I had finished eating it, despite how I had to keep forcing myself to take it down my esophagus, I felt full and a little content.

Rita's hand looked for mine once I had finished cleaning my plate and cutlery. "We need to talk about Angelo."

I retracted my hand gently and groused, "No, I don't want to talk about him. It's over. I'm not going to marry Angelo. I loved father and all, but I don't want to marry a man that lied to me this whole time."

I was going to pace to the backyard when she grabbed my hand again and halted me.

Her grip was firm.

It was certain.

She had something even more important than everything she'd told me thus far, and she was intent on making me hear her out.

I couldn't help but peer at her.

Her eyes were just as certain as her grip.

And when Rita spoke the first word, I knew it was going to be hard not to be convinced.

CHAPTER 17

Don't Believe in Lies

Angelo

I did the right thing. Alide broke up with me and now she could find someone much better for her – a man capable of giving her a child I couldn't. That's what comforted me right now.

She could now have a better boyfriend.

And then, a husband.

And as many children as she wanted.

I pulled the trigger, shattering another beer bottle to pieces. I took another drag off my cigarette and couldn't help but admire the One World Trade Center Building in the distance. It was shining like a beacon.

It could almost be interpreted as hope.

But I didn't believe I had any.

I put my finger on the trigger again when I heard the soft sound of someone's footsteps.

"Hey, boss."

It was Prudenzio. He lifted his hand over his head as if to tell me he had come in peace. We weren't in bad terms or anything like that. I just didn't feel like talking to anyone tonight.

The stars were shining like diamond shards in the sky. Picturesque in their existence, and reminding me just how small I was and how nothing of what was happening here mattered to the rest of the universe.

"Hey," I said, lowering the beer bottle and putting it on the step of the stands I was sitting on, or whatever it was called. It stood in front of an abandoned soccer field, or at least, that's what I'd deduced after finding this place.

The grass was long and marked with spots where it had long stopped growing. The white lines which were supposed to delineate the limits of the field were also faded, like nobody cared about this place anymore.

It almost reminded me of me.

"I heard what happened..." Prudenzio murmured, leaving me to fill in the blanks.

"I thought I was doing the right thing, and in a way, I did." I swallowed, feeling my throat dry. "There's something about me you need to know."

Before now, I would never have considered telling him this. However, things were different now.

Prudenzio said nothing, merely looking ahead as if the Manhattan skyline had been put there by aliens.

I drew in some air and continued, "I'm infertile. I can't gift Alide a child of our own. She did the right thing by breaking up with me." I paused. "And now she can find someone better for her."

I thought he wasn't going to say anything, but he immediately spoke.

"Does that even matter, Angelo? She was happy with you without even thinking about ever getting pregnant. Shouldn't that be the only thing that truly matters?"

He snapped his head to me, eyes locking. That resolve in his eyes... I'd never seen it before.

I didn't talk to him much about my relationship with Alide, but it seemed he knew quite a bit about it. I also got the impression it mattered a lot to him.

"I know that maybe I shouldn't be telling you this," he continued, "but she was changing you. She was making you better, and as your friend, I can't not help you."

I valued him helping me cope with the breakup, but I didn't think there was anything I could do to mend things. She didn't want to see me again. She made that known the instant she barged out of the Bello Italiano.

"It's over anyway," I started to say. "There is nothing I can do to change her mind."

"That's where you are wrong. You think I don't know what you are going through?" His eyes grew intense, like he was remembering a wound of his past. "Talk to her again. Go to her house. Make her hear what you've got to tell her."

I waved my hand. "I don't think that will help. At most she will kick me out of there and call the cops on me."

He shook his head, and that's when I knew I was only telling myself what was going to make me feel better. In other words, fooling myself again.

He stood up and situated himself in front of me.

His eyes were burning with his intention to fix everything that was wrong.

And I knew I couldn't do anything to change his mind.

Because... I was sure he was going to make me alter my decision.

Alide

The bus bumped each time it drove over a pothole. I turned my head to look out the window and couldn't help but think about how Rita was just... *right*. I didn't even hear him out when I barged through him and rushed back home. I'd presumed he had betrayed me for his own benefit.

But it wasn't the case. He kept it hidden all this time for a good reason, and I trusted him. Maybe he was just misguided.

Considering all these moments we had together, I should at least have given him the benefit of the doubt. Rita didn't convince me he was a good man after all the things he did, but she did make me come back to him.

It was dark outside and I had no idea if he was still in the Bello Italiano, but I felt I was doing the right thing, and I wasn't going to stop for anything until I was with him again.

To make things right, I was willing to meet him, regardless of the consequences.

To try to understand his reasons, it was worth going there when I had no idea how things were going to pan out.

My heart and mind were in chaos, but still... This was the fair thing to do.

I was all alone on the bus. It was crossing the Brooklyn bridge now, heading to Little Italy. The stars were now covered by some clouds, and the light of the moon could barely breach them.

The bus then stopped, and I started walking to the Bello Italiano. Maybe I should have called him first, but I didn't have the stomach for that. It didn't feel right to talk to him over the phone about something so important.

My legs were like gelatin as I crossed the sidewalk and then floundered my way to the Bello Italiano.

The sign was standing in the distance, turned off and looking as if it was dead.

I thought I'd never come back here.

A shadow then dashed out of nowhere, and a gun clicked.

It was *him*.

And I knew that face.

"You are coming with me."

Angelo

I had no idea Prudenzio could be so convincing when he wanted to. I didn't ask him about it, but I was sure he was seeing in me something that had happened to him a long time ago. He didn't want to let it happen again.

I was grateful I had him as my friend.

He was so much more than the soldier I'd been bringing with me to hunt down Vinicio.

He did the right thing, and I now I felt I had to do the same. I had to try talking to Alide again.

One more time.

Just one more time.

Maybe I could make it right. Maybe? No. Unquestionably. I could make it right. Screw being infertile. Screw the marriage.

All she needed was my open heart.

I opened the door to get into the car and my phone buzzed. I fished it out of my pocket and thought about the random number that was calling me. Typically, that meant it was someone who dialed the wrong number, which was pretty common in a city as populous as New York.

I glanced at Prudenzio, who was still with me. We hadn't left the area where the abandoned soccer field resided yet, and I was just about to call Alide to ask her if we could meet up first before the phone buzzed.

I wasn't going to just pop up at her place uninvited again without knowing how she would take seeing me one more time.

I tapped on the green button and put the phone by my ear.

And that's when I knew that, more than ever before, the love of my life needed me. And she needed me *right fucking now.*

* * *

He'd asked me to come here alone, and I did. It was an old warehouse just on the edge of the city. Nobody lived nearby, and nobody would ever find out what was about to transpire in here.

The moon was just setting in the distance, and soon the sun was going to be casting its light on New York. The stars were fading back behind the growing blueness of the sky. It wouldn't be long until it was a new day.

And I was just hoping Alide was going to come back alive.

I didn't care about my life.

I came here to save her.

This one moment, I decided to do the right thing.

I didn't want to be a quitter ever again.

I came to this old, decrepit warehouse without a gun. I didn't tell Prudenzio about the call. I told him it was my father who had called me to come back home, and he believed me.

I felt a little bad I lied to him, but it was the right thing to do. He then headed somewhere. I didn't ask him where he was going, though. To be honest, I didn't care. All I knew was that I needed to rescue Alide.

Footsteps rounded a corner, and a man with a woman in front of him showed up. Vinicio and Alide. I couldn't despise him for what he was doing. The look in his eyes... It showed how desperate he was.

And he wasn't smiling.

His mouth was deformed, like he was hating himself for doing this.

And I could understand his reasons.

He ran away from our family because he didn't want to hurt anyone. But ever since then, it was all he did. He almost killed me, harmed other citizens, consorted with the Ancelottis, and was now keeping an innocent woman hostage.

I had no idea he knew about me and her.

He must have been seeking this whole time for a chance to kidnap her.

That was his only way to get himself out of the city, right?

He halted, his hand holding a pistol to Alide's head. She looked unharmed, but she had a gag in her mouth. She tried to speak and struggle, but Vinicio was stronger than her.

Vinicio's clothes were worn and holes littered it. That stench too. It had been a long time since he took a shower. Not a surprising thing, to be honest, considering how long he had been on the run.

His best friend also told us all he had on him. We were this close to capturing him, and now I was throwing all that away for a chance to make things right for once.

To save Alide, I was willing to do anything and everything.

She looked alright for the most part. No bruises or cuts. She wasn't harmed by him, and that was good.

I'd never forgive him otherwise.

He was holding her to him like she was something dangerous that could decimate New York if she were let loose, and that made my blood boil.

I didn't want to hate my brother, but he was testing my patience right now.

I was kneeling in front of him, and had my hands behind my head.

I did it just like he wanted.

He made it all pretty clear.

If I didn't obey his orders, I knew he meant it when he said Alide wasn't going to come out of this alive.

And for her, I was willing to sacrifice myself.

"Give me your word you are going to let me escape the city. You make it happen, she will live."

"I give you my word. I'm not going to hunt you down again. I'll set up something for you in one of our checkpoints."

"That won't do!" He barked, shaking the hand with the pistol. "You are taking me with you in the trunk of your car."

"Okay, Okay," I breathed in and out, hard. "I'll do anything. Just don't harm her."

"And there's more. She'll come with us, and you will leave a car just past the border after you drop me off. I can't risk anything. I have to consider all the details. I know you want to kill me."

"I won't try that, and I'm going to do everything you are asking."

His voice was alarmed, like his mind was finally envisioning a possible escape from New York.

It was just like he said.

One thing he did wrong and he could end up finding himself in our father's grasp.

"She'll be in the trunk with me. Call one of your soldiers to leave a vehicle past the border, and now walk with me to your car. We are doing this now."

A moment of unnerving silence.

"You want her alive, right?"

I nodded. My eyes locked with his. Despite the gravity of this, I was calm and composed. I finally made up my mind. Vinicio didn't even have to push me hard to make me do what he wanted.

I understood him.

I wanted him to flee.

That would be much better than letting father have him locked in a dark room.

"Stand up and walk with me. Drive, *and no funny ideas.* I'll pull the trigger if I feel you are going to betray me again."

With my hands still clasped behind my head, I slowly stood up and locked my eyes with Alide. She was scared. It was as clear as day. She'd never been in a situation like this.

And more than anything right now, I hated myself.

Had she never involved herself with me, she would be alright at this moment.

She would have the money and the treatment for Luca, and a good job so that she could continue providing for him.

I nodded to her.

She needed that reassurance.

I was going to get her out of this one way or another.

If Vinicio's plan had a flaw or not, I couldn't figure it out. Despite being calm, my mind could think of one thing only.

To get Alide out of this.

And to tell her how much my love for her meant to me.

I padded to the car and Vinicio followed me, his arm still holding Alide tightly. I then heard an explosion and a scream. My heart skipped a beat.

He couldn't have done it.

I gave him no reason to believe I was lying.

I was merely walking to my car like he'd asked.

I spun around and found Alide thrown on the ground, her hands trying to get the gag off her mouth.

Vinicio was shrieking as his gun slid on the cement floor far away from him. His hands were covering a wound in his leg, and he was bleeding. A lot.

His expression was one of absolute pain.

And I had no idea what'd just happened.

All I could think of was to get Alide out of this.

I sprinted to her and helped her take off the gag. Her eyes locked with mine and I believed I could read what she was thinking.

But the moment of clarity turned out to be short-lived.

Vinicio was crawling to his gun.

He was thinking I did this.

He was going to get his gun and shoot us dead, and I didn't bring any weapon with me – just like he demanded on his call.

I put Alide's arm around my shoulders. She couldn't walk by herself right now. The mental trauma of being kidnapped was too much for her.

More than anything, I detested myself.

She would never ever be here if she hadn't fallen in love with me.

I was right about my world and hers being too different.

I was far too hazardous to her.

Vinicio was still crawling to his gun when a man's voice roared, "Stop right there, or I'll put a bullet through your head this time."

My head snapped to the direction his voice came from. My eyes picked up a glint and the long barrel of a sniper rifle. Behind it was standing the guy who had just saved me.

And he was none other than Prudenzio.

A surge of warmness flooded my heart.

I had no idea he'd followed me here. I didn't want to involve him because I didn't want to give Vinicio a reason to think I wasn't going to be truthful to my word.

Risking Alide's life wasn't a choice I could have made.

And now, with her hugging me, and Vinicio on the floor, I knew I could make things right.

It didn't have to end the way our father wanted.

And I was going to make use of this opportunity to show Vinicio I wasn't like him.

He was going to live his life the way he desired.

CHAPTER 18

Letting it All Go

Angelo

I embraced Vinicio and patted his back passionately. "Father can't find you now."

He smiled, not believing it was finally happening.

Likewise, I couldn't believe I was helping him escape after chasing for so long. But things changed, and they did for the better.

"Thank you, my brother." He paused. "I'm sorry I kidnapped Alide."

I didn't say anything. Not all of this felt right. I couldn't absolve him for the things he did, but I could understand he was desperate. I pushed him too far. A couple more days, after all, and he wouldn't have been able to escape our grasp again.

I nodded and stated, "I'll tell father you escaped on your own."

He bowed slowly, comprehending I had to tell a lie to my father, or that else he was going to have to put his men to pursue him throughout the country.

Just when he was going to turn, I grabbed my pistol and offered it to him.

"Take it. You are going to need it more than me."

His eyes surveyed the gun like he couldn't believe I was doing this. It had been mine for a long time. Father gave it when I turned 18. It meant a lot to me, but I needed to get rid of it now.

Alide was with us, her hand around my lower back. She was so close to me I could hear her breathing, despite the roaring of the cars on the highway. We were just outside the city. Manhattan stood in the distance, and the sun was casting long shadows all throughout the province we were in.

His hand grabbed the gun and then put it in his waistband. "Thank you. I'm not going to forget this."

He turned and ambled to the car I'd left for him.

And since then, I never saw him again.

Alide's arm enveloping my lower back was the only thing that comforted me. I guessed that one way or another I was always going to lose Vinicio. At least this way he had a chance to have a normal life.

He would have to get himself a fake ID and keep his guard up all the time, but it was better than being hunted down by the Mafia.

And father would believe me.

I never lied to him before, after all.

And he always knew Vinicio was talented enough to fool me and the rest of the family.

Him finally escaping was an outcome he'd always considered likely.

EPILOGUE

Alide

Being with Angelo again just felt right. I couldn't blame him anymore for what he did. I understood his reasons, and we talked about them. He didn't think I'd take the marriage well. How could I have thought my father wanted me to marry the heir of a don?

Back when I learned the truth, it felt like he'd been lying to me that whole time, and he had been. That's something I couldn't pretend otherwise.

He did keep the truth concealed, and I was in the right to have felt the way I did.

Still, now I understood his reasons, and they made sense.

He hadn't been courageous enough to reveal the plans for the wedding to me, and he reckoned it would destroy all the things that made me who I was.

But I forgave him.

I couldn't continue to pretend I didn't love him anymore.

I did, and love was such a blind and intense feeling.

It didn't matter if he'd kept the truth hidden.

What mattered was that he regretted his choice, and was now eager to make everything right.

I unlinked my arm from Rita's and padded to him. I'd never worn a heeled sandal like this one, but for a place like this – this church – it was more than required. I'd never put on a dress like this one as well.

Everything was so unfamiliar to my eyes.

The dress was bigger than what I'd seen in some movies, and so white there wasn't even a speck of dust on it. Angelo made sure I was going to have the best for the marriage, and he was truthful to his word.

This felt right.

This felt what I wanted the most for my life.

Rita and Luca were now sitting on one of the front benches. She was using a handkerchief to wipe her tears while my little brother watched the scene in front of him with the utmost devotion.

He's never been in a marriage, and so it was no wonder he was flabbergasted.

The church, which was located in Lower Manhattan, was of baroque design and origin. The outside and the inside of it composed a piece of art difficult to find elsewhere in the country, and more than anything, it was right for this moment.

I'd wanted to marry Angelo since I fell in love with him.

And now, he was going to become my spouse.

I padded to him, and some people were still finding their seats and talking. That gave us some minutes to talk.

His eyes were gleaming with joy, and likewise, I couldn't contain my racing heart. It was as if everything was happening in slow motion to me.

I was taking in all the details of the wedding.

This was one of those things I would never forget.

His hands grabbed mine as he said, "You look undeniably beautiful."

I giggled gently. "And you look so gorgeous in that outfit."

A moment of pause as I took in his expression of happiness mixed with love. I couldn't stop gazing at his lips and eyes. They were the most charming I'd seen in my whole life, and right now, I wanted to kiss him so much.

And I was conscious it wasn't the right time.

But we were going to marry anyway, and who said I needed to follow every wedding custom.

It was with that thought in mind I pulled Angelo to me and sealed my lips with his.

The crowd in the church echoed their surprise mixed with shock, and all I could do was to continue kissing him.

I made the right choice, and I was never going to leave him for anything.

Angelo chose me to be his.

And I elected him to be my eternal husband.

The End

ABOUT THE AUTHOR

Jolie Damman lives with her puppies and many cats on her farmland. She enjoys spending time with nature and tending to her property. When she has some free time, which doesn't happen as often as she would like, she writes her books.

As a writer, she hopes to touch and change the heart of her readers. Her books are not for those weak of the heart, and they tend to be spicier than most. One word after the other, she doesn't stop typing until she has written her idea, and she is very desire-driven when it comes to establishing the connections of her characters.

www.ingramcontent.com/pod-product-compliance
Lightning Source LLC
Chambersburg PA
CBHW051437140726
47987CB00006B/2409